For the Love of Animals

Elise Noble

Published by Undercover Publishing Limited

ISBN: 978-1-910954-81-2

Edited by Nikki Mentges, NAM Editorial

www.undercover-publishing.com

www.elise-noble.com

For Gigi.

FOREWORD

If you've read any of my other books, you may have noticed I've got a soft spot for animals, and I'm thrilled to be able to raise money to help the dogs, cats, and horses of Janet's Wadi in Dahab, Egypt with these stories—three tales of how our furry friends can bring people together in sometimes unusual ways.

And, of course, there's a little bit of Blackwood...

Dali the Dog

Chapter 1 - Carmen

OUCH. WHATEVER BUG was crawling over my ankle bit me again, and I cursed under my breath. But I couldn't swat it. Not when two of Miguel Lozano's guards were looking in my direction. The slightest movement could give my position away, our mission would be compromised, and *mi abuela* would cry big, messy tears at my funeral.

I squinted through my rifle scope again as the thinner of the two guards laughed and lit a cigarette. Didn't he know those things killed people? Although granted, the life expectancy of Lozano's henchmen wasn't long.

And me? I might just die of boredom.

If I did, what would they tell my mother? She hadn't wanted me to join the army in the first place, so I'd told a small fib and now she thought I worked in the kitchen, cooking meals for the troops. *I'm sorry, Señora Hernandez, Carmen accidentally cut an artery and bled to death while preparing burritos.*

As the only woman in a twenty-person team seconded out of GAFE High Command, the most elite group in Mexico's Special Forces, I had one job, and that was to shoot people. Literally, one job. When I'd joined the group, I'd hoped for so much more, but despite the men at the top going on about equal opportunities, I'd been bashing my head off the glass ceiling for a year now while laughing off sexist "banter" and pretending I didn't care when my colleagues patted me on the ass.

And the question was, did I want it to continue? I'd nearly completed five years, and my contract was up in a month. Everyone just assumed I'd sign up for another stint. Including me, until our new commanding officer had arrived two months ago, a hurried replacement after the previous one got arrested for corruption. After our beloved new leader made it very clear I'd never be considered an equal, I'd christened him Captain Pendejo. While the men trained in the latest counterterrorism techniques, I was expected to be on the range day in, day out, round after round. I loved my guns, don't get me wrong, but sometimes I just wanted a little variety.

What would I do if I quit? There wasn't much call for snipers outside the military. Perhaps I could retrain as a secretary or a realtor or a nurse? You know, keep people alive for a change. Or a dog groomer. I liked dogs.

A puppy lay on Lozano's veranda, snoozing in the sun. The poor thing was so skinny I could count her ribs through my scope, but she wouldn't get any love from Lozano's men—one of them had already kicked her as he walked past. Asshole. I'd followed him with my crosshairs, finger on the trigger, imagining what would happen if I squeezed just a tiny bit harder. With the high-velocity rounds I used, his head would have exploded.

But I had to let him walk. Today, I'd been assigned to a last-minute job by Captain P after our number-one sniper got shot—oh, the irony—and all I could do was watch from six hundred yards while my so-called partner, José, got the job of infiltrating the villa and killing Lozano and his second in command, a three-hundred-pound motherfucker they called *el antílope*. The freaking antelope. *El elefante* would have been more appropriate.

José had disappeared inside four hours ago, and I hadn't moved since. Backache was part of the job. What was he doing in there? Every so often, muffled footsteps or a snippet of conversation came through my earpiece, but he never bothered giving me an update. He had a plan, he'd assured me back at base, although he didn't care to share the details. My instructions were simple: if Lozano or *el antílope* showed their faces outside the villa, shoot them then exfiltrate the scene. Yes, I'd truly felt like a valued member of the team after that back-of-an-envelope briefing.

The puppy got up, stretched, and meandered into the house, careful to give *el cabrón* in the lawn chair a wide berth. Kind of wished I could do the same.

Crack.

A gunshot sounded in stereo, almost deafening me. A single groan followed, then silence.

"José?"

Nothing.

"José? Are you there?"

Was he dead or just unable to speak? Shouts came from the house, and the man in the lawn chair ran inside. Should I stay or leave? If José had been killed, I was a sitting duck because Lozano's men would surely find his earpiece and look for an accomplice. But if he was alive and I left him, I could be signing his death warrant. And what if he was injured? Should I try to help? This. *This* was why we needed proper briefings.

A crackle sounded through my earpiece, and for a moment hope blossomed in my chest, but then my heart stuttered.

"Nobody tries to kill me and gets away with it. *El antílope* is coming for—"

Another gunshot, silenced this time, followed by a voice growling, "Fuck you, elephant man."

That wasn't José, definitely not. This man sounded American, but Lozano didn't have any Americans in the house. Didn't trust them.

So who was he? If my assumptions were correct, *el antílope* had shot José, and then the mysterious stranger had shot *el antílope*. Instinct told me to get out of there, but curiosity got the better of me as a muffled *boom* shook the far side of the house.

I stayed put.

Smoke curled from the roof as Lozano's limousine accelerated down the driveway. Dammit—our main target was escaping, and there was no point in taking a shot. That vehicle had bulletproof glass, armoured bodywork, and run-flat tyres. Nothing short of an army would get Mexico's número uno drug dealer out of his car, and they'd be swimming in blood while they did it.

Back at the house, a dark figure appeared in the doorway beside the veranda, framed by wisps of smoke as he scanned left and right. Behind him, flames licked at the furnishings as the fire destroyed one overly ostentatious home and about eighteen million dollars' worth of coke, if our estimates were correct. Lozano used the proceeds to finance terrorist campaigns against the government, among other things, so the blaze probably saved as many lives as it took.

I trained my crosshairs on the guy, but before I could take a shot, he ducked back inside. Why? I soon got my answer. When he reappeared, he was stuffing something inside his jacket. Something wriggly. The puppy. He'd gone back for the puppy. And while he was on his rescue mission, he hadn't noticed lawn-chair-guy creeping around the side of the house, eyes fixed on the doorway.

The stranger was quick, I'd give him that. He got his gun up before LCG managed to fire, and we had ourselves a standoff.

A good old Mexican standoff.

Now I had a choice. I could kill Lozano's man, or the gringo who'd quite possibly just fucked up our operation, or both of them. I trained my scope on the stranger, and a flicker of recognition hit. I'd seen him before at the base, and recently too. Not one of our people, but a visitor. I'd caught him staring at me in the canteen the other day, the pig, but when I glared at him, he'd looked away instead of making a lewd gesture like guys usually did. In my head, I'd called him *huevitos*. Little balls. When I asked around, Captain P's secretary told me he was here from Washington, DC to deliver a course on hostage negotiation, the course I wasn't allowed to go on because I had breasts.

And now it seemed our American friend had decided to combine business with pleasure.

A sigh escaped my lips as I inched my barrel to the right and shot LCG between the eyes. He went down like a bad taco—satisfying but kind of messy.

One blink and *huevitos* had disappeared, but it didn't matter. I'd find him later.

CHAPTER 2 - CARMEN

GETTING CHEWED OUT by Captain Pendejo—my absolute favourite activity on a swelteringly hot Monday morning.

"For the last time, I was six hundred yards away, so I didn't see what happened, and José didn't keep me updated. All I know is that he got into an altercation with *el antílope* and neither of them came out of the house alive."

"For the last time, *Cabo* Hernandez, this isn't good enough." He called me Corporal like an insult. "How am I supposed to explain to my superiors that the mission failed?"

"It succeeded in part. One of our targets died." Although I very much suspected José hadn't done much to achieve that. "And we can still go after Lozano."

Captain P paced his office, up and down, up and down, up and down. How did he get the creases in his pants so sharp? Either he spent more time ironing than working or some poor woman had to do it for him. Ugh. The idea of being married to a man like that was enough to make me reach for the chastity belt.

Then he stopped, and I didn't like the way he grinned at me. A cunning expression, and one that suggested I didn't want to hear what he was about to say.

"Okay, here's what we'll do. You always say you want more responsibilities? New challenges? Then you kill Lozano yourself."

"But—"

"One week. I can hold them off for one week. I'll tell them that we're halfway to completion and now we're reverting to our backup plan."

"Do we have a backup plan?"

He opened both arms to me. "Time to prove yourself, Hernandez. I don't want to see you back here until this time next week."

His unspoken words? If I didn't complete the task, he didn't want to see me back there ever. I saw right through him, all the way to his slimy little soul. He'd always resented having a woman on the team, having to make allowances with regards to accommodation and a specially tailored uniform, and this was his chance to get rid of me. If I failed at this job, he could claim I wasn't capable of keeping up with the boys.

"Absolutely. Leave it with me. Can I get any assistance?"

"Since this assignment should be finished already, everyone else is busy. You'll have access to our regular intelligence sources, of course."

"Thanks so much."

He didn't pick up on the sarcasm, just waved me towards the door.

"I look forward to reading your report, Cabo."

Where did I start? I'd never had to plan and execute a

job alone before. Haha—execute. Do you like what I did there? Yes, I'd asked to progress at work, but I'd hoped to ease into a more challenging role gently rather than getting tossed in at the deep end. The deep end of a volcano filled with bubbling lava.

Eliminate Lozano in only one week? It was a suicide mission. After the failed attempt yesterday, his security would have been tightened, and it had been tough to penetrate before. The man never travelled anywhere without a dozen bodyguards surrounding him, and with the men on high alert, his two remaining properties would be locked down like fortresses. He always carried a gun himself, and we had it on good authority that he'd acquired a rocket launcher on the black market last year.

And it wasn't only Lozano I had to deal with. I also needed to have a chat with *huevitos*, and worse, my presence was required at my grandma's seventy-eighth birthday celebration. The celebration she was treating more like a wake because some crazy psychic told her she only had a week left to live.

I decided to tackle the lesser of the three evils first. "Little balls" couldn't be that bad if he'd saved a puppy, right? The only question was, where was he staying? Not on base—I'd seen him arrive in a black SUV one morning and park in a visitor space.

Nestor, one of my less misogynistic colleagues, raised a hand in greeting as I walked past, but I kept going because I didn't feel like rehashing my failures. My target, Captain P's secretary, grimaced at her screen for a moment then looked up at me.

"You survived?" she asked.

"Barely."

"I was worried—yesterday, the boss turned a horrible shade of red and I thought he might have a heart attack."

Shame he didn't. "He seems to be calm now, but he asked me to take on an extra project. Do you happen to know where I can find that hostage negotiation guy? Apparently, he's got the files I need."

"The course is finished, but he mentioned sticking around for some sightseeing. Hold on, I'll see if I can find his details..."

Sightseeing. Right. Because every tourist wanted to take a selfie with a dead drug dealer.

"Ah, here it is. Nathaniel Wood." She jotted the address of a nearby apartment onto a scrap of paper. "Shall I call and let him know you're coming?"

"No, I'll surprise him." And also change the subject. "How did your trip to Cancún go?"

"Oh, it was amazing! We stayed—"

My phone rang, and I'd never been so glad to get interrupted by my mother. No, honestly. Usually, I avoided her calls at all costs.

"Excuse me. Family problems."

The secretary nodded, and I hurried into the hallway, relieved and worried at the same time.

"Mamá, what is it?"

"Good news, *chiquita*. I know you've been so busy over the past few weeks, so I've found you a date for your grandma's party."

"You've what? Who?"

"Gerardo Pineda. You're perfect for each other. You love to cook, and he loves to eat."

Yes, and it showed. I'd gone to school with Gerardo and he'd been shovelling down everything in sight since first grade. When he chewed, his jaw made this funny clicking noise like a deathwatch beetle. It might have been fascinating if it weren't so freaky.

"I can't go with Gerardo Pineda."

"Why? He's got a good job, Carmen. There's always a call for accountants."

Yes, even drug dealers had them. Lozano's man was a smarmy asshole who walked with a limp after getting shot in the knee three years ago. I'd done well that day.

"He's just not my type."

"You're not getting any younger, *chiquita*."

"I'm only twenty-three, Mamá."

"Gloria next door got married at twenty-one, and now she's got two babies. If you don't get a move on, all the good men will be gone. Gerardo's offered to take you out next Saturday too, and his mother says he always picks somewhere good for the first date."

Like an all-you-can-eat buffet? "Mamá, I have a boyfriend."

Why did I say that? I clapped one hand over my mouth so no more stupid, stupid words fell out. Desperation made my brain malfunction.

"You do?" Why did she sound so surprised? "That's wonderful! Is it serious?"

"I'm not sure yet."

Just like I wasn't sure whether to jump off the nearest bridge or hurl myself in front of a passing truck.

"Never mind. We all look forward to meeting him on Tuesday. Can you make your chicken tamale pie? You know how much your grandma likes it."

"No problem."

"I'll get your room ready too. You are staying the

night, aren't you?"

"Sure."

"Your grandma's calling—see you soon, *chiquita.*"

No problem? Right. *Everything* was a problem. The only deep and meaningful relationship in my life right now was with my Accuracy International AWM, chambered in Lapua Magnum .338 for extra range, but it didn't do so well with small talk.

Now I had two big challenges: find a date for Grandma's party and kill Lozano. Maybe I really should have gone into catering.

CHAPTER 3 - NATE

"YOU DID WHAT?" Black asked. He'd called Nate from Virginia for an update. "You went to blow up a drug dealer and came back with a puppy?"

Black was a grumpy fucker who rarely smiled, but right now, he was laughing so hard he could barely speak. Nate sat on the floor in his rented studio apartment and groaned as the dog pissed on the tiles again.

"The thing was hiding under a chair. I couldn't just leave it there to barbecue."

"Remember the time I went to England to waste a businessman and came back with an eighteen-year-old brat in tow?"

How could Nate ever forget? Emmy—the girl Black was training as an assassin—had driven him insane for months. Still did, but at least she was good at her job now.

"Yeah, I remember."

"Well, you might actually have beaten that. What are you gonna do, train the mutt to sniff for explosives?"

"Who the fuck knows? It's more interested in licking its own ass at the moment. What the hell am I supposed to do with it?"

"Take it to the shelter and make a donation?"

"I'll see if there's one nearby."

"More importantly, what about Lozano? And who was the other guy in the house?"

"No idea, but he hadn't done his homework. Everyone else knew *el antílope* took a nap in the afternoon. I'll have to go at Lozano again, but it'll be tougher this time. My informant died in the crossfire."

Dammit, Nate had almost had Lozano and his whole team. Another half hour and he'd have planted enough charges to blow the entire villa and all of its occupants sky high, the informant would have left, and Lozano would have been toast. Instead, Nate had been forced into damage control mode.

And he'd nearly lost his fucking head.

He didn't plan on telling Black about the standoff outside because the man never made a mistake. They'd been best friends for years, swim buddies in the Navy SEALS before switching to an elite unit at the CIA and finally starting Blackwood Security together, but he couldn't help feeling inferior sometimes. Black cruised through life, effortlessly destroying anything that got in his way. A cyborg. Although he'd become a little more humanoid since Emmy appeared on the scene.

Then there was the question of the sniper. Someone had taken out the asshole who ambushed Nate, and he hadn't hung around to find out who. Now curiosity was eating away at him. Unless the shooter's aim was off, he hadn't been one of Lozano's men, and Nate's mystery saviour seemed too competent to have been with the prick *el antílope* had shot in the villa. Lozano had a list of enemies longer than *War and Peace*, and narrowing it down would take Nate time he didn't have. But continuing with the job while an unknown killer lurked on the periphery left him twitchy.

"So, we're going with Plan B now?" Black asked.

"Looks like it." Nate had hoped to avoid the need for that, because the B stood for Black—he'd come up with the idea, Nate had refined it, and as usual, it was fucking twisted. "But I'll have to keep a low profile because now Lozano's whole team's gonna be on the lookout for a single male matching my description."

"Want to borrow Emmy?"

Black was joking, but Nate was actually tempted to take him up on the offer.

"I'll let you know."

"Do that. I can have her on a plane in half an hour."

Something about Black's tone made Nate hesitate. "Is it that time of the month again?"

"Possibly. She almost took my head off in the boxing ring this morning."

"Why don't you keep her?"

Black just laughed and hung up, right as somebody knocked on the door. Nate's hand flew straight to the gun at his hip. Who was there? He wasn't expecting anyone.

"Shh," he told the puppy. "Good dog. Go in the bathroom."

With the mutt shut away, he stood to one side of the door. It had a peephole, but using it would be suicide if there was someone who wanted to kill him on the other side.

"Who is it?"

A pause. "Carmen Hernandez. I work at GAFE High Command. Captain P... Captain Benitez sent me with some paperwork."

"What kind of paperwork?"

"I don't know. It's in an envelope. You're Nathaniel Wood, yes?"

Nate cracked the door open, and sure enough, the brunette he'd seen in the mess hall the day before yesterday stood there. The hot one who'd made his dick twitch then stared him down when she caught him looking. But she was empty-handed.

"Nate Wood. So, where's the envelope?"

"There isn't one. I just wanted to talk to you."

She did? At lunch, he'd asked the guy sitting next to him about her, but he'd just shaken his head. "Don't waste your time with Carmen," he'd said. "The colonel panicked and hired her after the army got hit with a sexism lawsuit. Great shooter, but she's frigid as fuck."

But now she was standing on Nate's doorstep, and up close, she looked even prettier. Smelled good too— some sort of flowers in her perfume or maybe her shampoo. His heart sped up as he inhaled again, and then he caught himself. What the fuck was he doing? Hell, if the SEALs had let women like Carmen in, he'd never have gotten any work done.

"Come in. Sorry the place is a mess. I wasn't expecting visitors."

"I'm surprised you're still here. Isn't your course finished now? Hostage negotiation, right?"

"Yeah, but I stuck around to catch up with friends."

She stepped inside and perched on the edge of the dining table, a flimsy thing made out of plastic that Nate hadn't eaten a single meal at.

"Friends? You mean friends like Miguel Lozano?"

Oh, shit. Nate stiffened, then forced himself to relax. *She's just fishing. She doesn't know anything.* She couldn't. Unless... What had the asshole in the mess hall said about her? That Carmen was a great shooter.

"I don't follow," he said.

Dark-brown eyes scanned the room, and she jerked her head in the direction of the bed.

"Do you pee on the floor often?"

That fucking dog. "I must have spilled a drink."

"Where's the puppy?"

"What puppy?"

She didn't answer, just listened, and the damn animal started whining on the other side of the bathroom door. Carmen rose gracefully and strode across the room before Nate could protest, and two seconds later, the mutt was leaping all over her. He should have been pissed at both of them, but when Carmen smiled for the first time, he forgot how to scowl.

"I suppose you're going to tell me you've never seen her before and you've got no idea how she got here?" Carmen said.

"Well, you obviously know. Which means you must have been the shooter on the grassy knoll."

She didn't try to deny it, just looked adorably confused for a second. "Grassy knoll?"

"Never mind. Why did you do it?"

Carmen gathered the dog up in her arms and sat on the edge of the bed. "He kicked the puppy. What have you named her?"

"Huh?"

"What have you named her?"

"No, the first part. You killed a man because he was mean to a dog?"

She shrugged, then nodded. Good grief. Nate made

a mental note to donate to the American Humane Society when he got home—there had to be some kind of karma at work.

"Her name?" Carmen prompted.

"Lady, I'm still trying to deal with the fallout from yesterday. The last thing I've had time to do is name a dog. Do you know where the nearest animal shelter is?"

She gasped. "You're getting rid of her?"

"What else am I meant to do? I'm in a foreign country with a job to do, which you're clearly aware of, and I don't have time to house-train our four-legged friend. I'm sure the shelter will find her a nice home."

"The local shelter is overflowing." Carmen tilted her head to one side, studying the puppy. "What sort of dog do you think she is?"

"I think she's a goat. She's already eaten one of my T-shirts and dumped the trash everywhere."

"Her face looks like a Basset Hound, but her body's more of a Hungarian Vizsla. I think she's gonna get bigger. Don't you think she's gonna get bigger?"

"Bigger? Great. How do you know so much about dogs?"

"I read a lot of books as a child. Dali. She looks like a Dali. See how her face is kind of droopy like those paintings with the clocks?"

"Fine, call her Dali, but I can't keep her. I have work to do."

"That's what I came to talk to you about. Your job is also my job, and I don't want you getting in the way."

Dali began licking Carmen's face, and Nate had never wanted to be a dog so much in his life, but he forced himself to snap out of his stupor. What was wrong with him? He didn't get distracted by women.

Not ever.

"*Your* job? You and your...partner?" She nodded, confirming his suspicions. "You and your partner already fucked it up once."

"Well, now it's just me, and I don't intend for that to happen again."

"You can't just shoot Lozano from a distance, you know. He's paranoid about that. Everywhere he goes, he's surrounded by bulletproof glass or bodyguards or both."

"Thank you, I've noticed."

Great, now Nate had insulted her. He didn't mean to, but he had to talk her out of going after Lozano. Not just because he was getting paid two million dollars to kill the man himself, but because he had doubts over her abilities and he didn't want her to get hurt. Her partner had already shown his lack of competence, and if she'd been trained in the same manner...

"So, what's your plan?" Nate asked.

"Why do you care who kills Lozano?"

"Money. Pride. Professional reputation. I don't like to let clients down."

"Why all the bullshit with hostage negotiation?"

"That's my day job. Lozano's more of a sideline. But stop trying to change the subject—what's your plan?"

"You think I'd tell you?"

"No, I think you don't have one."

Nate had expected more fight from her, but instead, she sagged forwards, cuddling Dali like a security blanket.

"I'll come up with something."

Or get herself killed. What if...? No, that was a stupid idea. But Nate's earlier words to Black repeated in his head. Lozano's men would be looking for a single man matching his description. But what if he wasn't alone?

"Why don't we work together?"

Carmen looked up at him, eyes wide. "Huh?"

"I said, why don't we work together?"

Chapter 4 - Carmen

I STUDIED NATE closely. Was he serious? He was, wasn't he?

"You say my partner messed up, but I've only got your word for that. How do I know you didn't get my colleague killed?" José might have been a sexist pig, but he'd completed many missions successfully. "You really think I want to work with you after that?"

"I was in the next room when your colleague was pissing around in *el antílope*'s suite. Didn't you realise the fat fuck took a nap each day at three p.m., regular as clockwork?"

Obviously not. "How do you know that?"

"Because I do my homework."

"Maybe so, but you still almost died."

Nate closed his eyes and groaned, and I took those few seconds to study him. Hair the colour of milk chocolate, café au lait skin, and when he looked at me again, irises the same dark brown as a strong espresso. The man was perfectly edible, and this time, it was my turn to groan. I should *not* have been thinking that way.

"Not my finest moment," he admitted. "But when the guards started searching the house, I had to get out of there. All I could do was blow the explosives I'd set and hope the blast got Lozano."

"And it didn't."

"No, it didn't."

This was weird. Discussing death with somebody outside my unit like it was normal, when the reality was anything but.

"Aren't you worried I might tell someone I saw you?"

"No."

"Why not?"

"I got away, remember? Firstly, you'd have to admit you compromised your operation when you got distracted by a dog, and secondly, I can produce three witnesses who'll swear blind I was drinking beer with them by the pool at the time of the incident. Perhaps you were mistaken?"

"You wouldn't..."

"Try me."

How had my life come to this? When I joined the army, I'd been determined to do good, to protect others from the fate that had befallen Juliana rather than offering thoughts and prayers every time another young woman got caught in the crossfire. Terrorists, drug lords, street gangs—none of them cared how many innocents got caught up in their wars.

I'd outscored most of my male colleagues on every test, come top of the class in marksmanship, and had more confirmed kills than any of them, but I still didn't have their respect. They never missed an opportunity to put me in my place, and Nate was no different. He played dirty.

Which left me no choice but to join in his game.

"I *do* have a plan."

"Can't wait to hear it."

"Let's take a trip to the range. One target, five hundred yards, ten rounds. If I win, you back off and let me take the lead on Lozano. If you win, I'll play sidekick."

"That's it? That's your plan?"

"Worried you'll lose?"

"No."

I liked his confidence. Totally misplaced confidence, but it was an attractive quality. *No, not attractive. Carmen!*

"Then let's go. Do you want to drive, or shall I?"

"You want to do this now?"

"Captain Benitez has given me until this time next week to deal with Lozano, so I can't afford to waste time. You have a gun, or do you need to borrow one?"

He hauled a bag out from under his bed. "I'll drive."

"What are you planning to do with Dali?"

"Shit. We'll have to leave her in the bathroom."

Shit? Absolutely she would. But Nate could clear the mess up when we got back, not me.

What did Nate have in the bag? I kept glancing across as he opened it, trying to act nonchalant as I assembled my own rifle. Inside, I felt twitchy, nervous. Not because I was scared of being outshot, but because I should have been plotting against Lozano and instead, I'd been forced into a stupid contest to get a man who didn't know when to quit off my back.

A CheyTac. He had a CheyTac Intervention, and yes, he had the .408 CheyTac ammo to go with it for extra precision. American made, that gun cost thirteen thousand dollars, so Nate must have been pretty successful at whatever he did even if he had screwed up the Lozano hit.

And the bad news for me was that the CheyTac had a longer range than my AWM, two thousand five hundred yards compared with my seventeen hundred, and for the first time since I suggested this contest, I began to feel a little nervous.

Block it out, Carmen. I had to trust in my own abilities.

Nate whistled as we sauntered down the range to pin our targets up. Two thick sheets of paper, each one printed with ten small black circles. He may have acted casual, but once I stretched out on the ground, I found comfort in familiarity—the *crack* of gunfire, the gentle westerly breeze, and the cool metal trigger against my finger as my world reduced to the view through my scope.

"Ladies first," Nate said.

If he insisted.

Crack. Dead centre.

"Nice shot."

Yes, it was.

I shifted sideways to watch him, and that stupid smirk disappeared as he focused on the target. He handled his rifle like the pro he was, and I cursed softly when his first bullet punched through the bullseye as well.

And so it went on. We matched each other shot for shot until the tenth, and I feared we'd end up in a stalemate. Nate was good, better than I'd suspected, and I was beginning to regret suggesting this match.

Relax. Stop breathing. Don't move anything except

your index finger. I lined up my crosshairs and exhaled, but just as I squeezed the trigger, Nate's foot touched mine. A bolt of electricity jolted through me, and the barrel jerked as I fired. My last round clipped the very edge of the target.

"You did that on purpose!"

"Did what?"

The smug grin was back, and I wanted to punch him in the face. "Kicked me, you asshole."

"Sorry. My foot must have slipped."

That...that... I hated him. How dare he walk into my life and try to turn it upside down? Perhaps he thought he was some hotshot assassin, and admittedly, he was right about the hot part, but that didn't mean he could ruin my career.

Not without consequences.

I waited until he lined up his shot, and just as the tension in his forefinger reached its maximum, I blew in his ear. He jumped and then cursed, glaring at me before he squinted through his scope.

"Outer ring. I win."

What? I checked myself, and my heart plummeted when I saw he was right. He'd hit the black, barely, but it still counted.

"You cheated."

"So did you."

"But since you started it, you had the element of surprise."

"War's unpredictable, Carmen. I'm thinking you need a sidekick costume. A short skirt, maybe some heels."

"And I'm thinking *you* need a slap."

"From you? I'd probably enjoy that."

Right then, I should have walked away. I should have told him where to stuff his costume and marched off with my head held high. But the part of me that still believed in honour wouldn't let me renege on the deal, and to my horror, a tear rolled down my cheek. Nate looked as shocked as I felt.

"Hey, I didn't mean to upset you."

"Yes, you did. Look, just give me a lecture about how assassins are supposed to be tough and get it over with, okay?"

Instead, he passed me a handkerchief. "I'm not gonna give you a lecture. You're a good shot. Better than I thought. How about a rematch instead?"

I peered at him suspiciously, but he almost looked sincere.

"What's the catch?" I asked. "I'm not wearing a leotard."

"Double or nothing. If I win, you have to help with Lozano plus find a home for the puppy."

"And if I win?"

"I don't know—pick something."

"Anything?"

"Sure. It's not like I'm gonna lose."

Oh, that arrogant... "Fine. I have a family dinner tomorrow evening, and I need someone to go with."

I admit it—I was desperate. Desperate enough to sit next to Nate for a whole hour if it kept my grandma happy.

Nate started laughing. "Like a date?"

"No! Definitely not a date. It's just that my family is under the mistaken assumption that I have a boyfriend, and I need to keep the pretence up."

"And you're single? I can't imagine why."

"You realise I'm holding a gun in my hands?"

"It's not loaded."

"If I hit you over the head with it, it'll still hurt."

"Okay, okay. Why do they think you've got a man?"

"I might have told my mother that when she tried to set me up with a *bicho raro*. Hey, stop laughing. It's not funny."

"You and a weirdo? It's funny from where I'm standing. Come on, pick something else. I'm not meeting your mom."

"I always knew you had *huevitos*."

"*Querida*, there's nothing small about my package."

"I think you're getting it confused with your ego."

"Just tell them the truth. That you're not interested in dating because you're too busy trying to shoot people." He stared at me for a second. "Wait—you haven't told them about your job either. Am I right?"

This time, I did walk off. If I was going to cry properly, I'd do it in the ladies' bathroom behind the range office—at least, if I could fit inside with all the broken junk they stored there.

"Hey, wait."

Nate put a hand on my arm, but I shook it off.

"Carmen, I didn't mean it. I'm sorry."

It was actually easier when he was an asshole. "Just leave me alone."

"Why does it matter so much? Lots of girls are single."

"Because all my grandma's ever wanted is to see one of her grandchildren get married. She's convinced she's only got a week left to live, and we've all let her down. My older sister died, my brother's gay and firmly locked in the closet, and I only seem to attract perverts and assholes."

"I'm sorry about your sister."

I shrugged, because if I let those emotions loose, I'd break down completely. "It happened six years ago."

"And your grandma? She's sick?"

"I don't think so. Honestly? I have no idea. My grandpa died a week after his seventy-eighth birthday, and some psychic predicted his death then told Grandma that she wouldn't live to be older than him."

"A psychic? You're serious?"

"Yes, and that isn't funny either. For the last six months, every headache's been a brain tumour, and if she coughs, it's SARS or pneumonia."

"Fifty bucks says she's still alive this time next week."

"What if she isn't? Her mental state's really fragile at the moment, and I want to keep her happy on her birthday."

Nate sighed and crouched to rummage through his duffel bag.

"Double or nothing, *querida*." He held up a handful of coins and a package of gum. "We'll play my game this time, and if you win, I'll help with Lozano and come to your family party. Deal?"

I didn't know whether to be nervous or relieved or happy or horrified. Mostly, I just felt sick. But as long as I didn't get distracted again, I could win—of that I was certain.

"Deal."

CHAPTER 5 - NATE

NATE STUCK A piece of gum in his mouth and chewed as he walked down the range. He'd officially lost his mind. Any sane man in his position would have taken the win, ignored the tears, and put his plan to assassinate Lozano into action.

But no, he'd shoved his hands into his pockets so he didn't get tempted to wipe Carmen's tears away, then given her another chance. She said she only attracted perverts and assholes? Which category did he fall into? Usually, he'd go with the latter, but the way his cock had hardened when she'd walked away from him definitely put him into pervert territory. That ass was enough to bring any man to his knees, and Nate wanted to track down whoever designed her skintight jeans and give them a medal.

Now he could feel her watching him, and he hoped she was getting a good eyeful, as Emmy would say. He spent long enough in the damn gym.

At the five-hundred-yard line he stopped, split his gum in two, and used it to stick two quarters upright on top of the target frame. At the seven-fifty line, he repeated the process with nickels, followed by dimes at a thousand yards. Then he walked back, using the time to ask himself what the hell he was doing.

The Lozano job was difficult enough without getting

distracted by a woman, but Carmen intrigued him. Not only was she beautiful, she was also a strange mix of strength and vulnerability, steel and silk, and he found himself wanting to challenge her as well as protect her. And fuck her. Okay, he admitted it. Earlier, he'd wanted to push her back on his bed and peel off that plain T-shirt she wore to keep herself hidden.

But he didn't, and he wouldn't, not unless she felt the same way. The way she eyed him nervously when he came close, her skittishness, suggested men hadn't been too kind to her in the past. And Nate knew for a fact that her commanding officer was a grade A douchebag because he'd had to speak to the man himself. Rumour said that Captain Benitez had been promoted due to nepotism—his godfather was a general—and Nate didn't see how else Benitez could have got to his position. His operational abilities were negligible, as were his people skills.

All of which had left Carmen miserable. Worse, Nate would bet his CheyTac that Benitez's loyalties didn't lie with the GAFE High Command, which didn't bode well for her future happiness either.

Nate wanted to see her smile.

"What are the coins for?" she asked, wary, although from the tone of her voice, she'd already guessed.

"Three coins each, three shots. Winner takes all."

"What happens if we both hit all three?"

"You think you're that good?"

"Yes."

At least she was confident in one area of her life.

"In that case, how about rock, paper, scissors?"

She rolled her eyes and chambered a round, then waved a hand at him. "You go first. How dirty are you planning to play this time around?"

Was this Nate's lucky day?

"We can get as dirty as you like, *querida*."

Nate loaded his gun and stretched out prone, lining the quarter up in his sights as he got into the right headspace. Back in the military, he'd spent many hours with Black as his spotter, focusing on targets as much as eighteen hundred metres away. At that distance, muzzle velocity plus wind speed and direction became crucial, and even breathing could make the difference between killing the target and missing completely.

Carmen settled beside him, leaving a gap of a foot. Near enough to be distracting, but still not as close as he'd like. He took aim, and just as he squeezed the trigger, she let out a piercing whistle.

Nice try. The quarter vanished.

"Gotta put in more effort than that, sweetheart."

"I'm not your sweetheart, or your *querida*, or anything else."

"Just a sore loser, huh?"

"I haven't lost."

"Yet."

Hmm, what to do first. Touching her was a bad idea, because as she'd pointed out, she had a gun in her hands and Nate quite liked his balls where they were. But she'd been the one to moot the possibility of playing dirty.

"Getting hot out here," he said, inching forwards.

She caught the movement out of the corner of her eye. "It's always hot. Wait, what are you doing?"

Nate peeled off his shirt and dropped it beside her, and yeah, she looked. He could bench-press four hundred pounds, and it showed.

Carmen's mouth set in a thin line, and she squinted through the scope. Paused. Flicked her gaze back towards him and shifted her position slightly. Uncomfortable. Good.

"You're an asshole, you know that?" she said.

Oh, he had her. "It's been mentioned a time or two."

Crack. The quarter flew off its chewing gum mount. Fuck, she was good. Better than good.

"Your turn."

Nate was more interested in what Carmen might come up with to distract him than the target, but he settled in behind his CheyTac. Until last year, he'd shot a Dragunov, an old Soviet-made design he'd grown fond of during a mission to assassinate a Ukrainian politician and make it look like the Russians did it. But Black had given him the CheyTac as a Christmas gift, and he had to concede it was more accurate.

Carmen's fingers curled around the hem of her top, a plain-black, no-nonsense T-shirt. No way. Surely she wasn't going to...

She did.

Nate couldn't even pretend to be interested in the fucking nickel as she peeled the shirt over her head and flung it at him. It was all he could do to stop himself from picking it up and sniffing it like a creeper.

But there were more important things to do, such as checking out the lady herself, now on her knees beside him in jeans and a sports bra. Flat stomach with a hint of muscle, breasts he wanted to dress up in something lacy then take pleasure in freeing later, and a face that would have been beautiful if its owner didn't look like she was sucking a hornet.

"Stop staring."

"*Querida*, you just undressed in front of me."

"Says the man standing there half-naked."

"I don't have a problem with you staring. Go right ahead."

"Just shoot the damn target, *cabrón*."

Crack. The nickel went flying, and Nate wasn't sure whether to be pleased or disappointed. His inner masochist wondered if going to Carmen's family party mightn't be an interesting experience.

"Your show, hotshot."

As Carmen settled onto her stomach, back arched, her golden skin glistening in the heat, Nate reached for his zipper. She glanced sideways, and her eyes widened as she did a double take.

"No! You can't do that!"

"Why not? Is it in the rules?"

"We're in public. Sort of."

"Then you'd better take your shot quickly."

Her head swivelled between him and the gun. Back and forth. Back and forth. Finally, she came to a decision.

Crack. Her nickel disappeared.

Good going. So, she could shoot under time pressure too.

Nate grinned at her and got rewarded with a flicker of a smile. Two points apiece, one shot left each. Was it bad that he was seriously considering missing on purpose? If he asked Carmen out for dinner, he bet she'd knock him back, so this family shitshow might be his only chance to spend time with her outside of work. Yes, losing would mean agreeing to take a back seat on Lozano too, but Nate already had a plan for that and it could tick along in the background while he convinced her to come around to his way of thinking. What about the dog? Surely Black knew someone who wanted a mutt—the man had connections everywhere.

The only thing getting in the way was Nate's pride. Did he really want to lose?

When Carmen reached over and squeezed his ass, he knew his answer. A small sigh escaped his lips as he moved the barrel a quarter inch to the right and fired.

"Dammit. I missed."

She still had her hand resting on his butt. "What? Really?"

"Yeah, but you still have to hit the dime. No big deal."

"Okay."

Now she bit her lip, and Nate realised she was more nervous now with a good shot at winning than before when she'd been the underdog. Carmen was a whole host of juxtapositions, all wrapped up in a perfect body. A woman in a man's world, proud of being there but also miserable. Confident in her own abilities yet worried she still wouldn't be good enough. Friendly yet prickly. Sexy as hell, yet she gave off this weird innocent vibe.

Nate was conflicted too. He enjoyed women's company, but he'd always avoided any kind of commitment. Now he found himself wondering what Carmen would think of the half-built farmhouse he was renovating back home in Virginia.

Shit, she was about to take her shot. Did he give her an easy ride or go all out to make her miss? He trailed one fingertip along her cheek, her skin soft and smooth under his touch. Black always said fate led him to

Emmy the night they met in London, and every time, Nate told him he was talking bullshit. But maybe the asshole was right and kismet really did exist?

Crack.

Carmen's squeal hurt Nate's ears, but her beaming grin made his dick harden.

"I got it." A pause, as if she couldn't quite believe what had happened. "I got it."

"Congratulations, *querida*. Now you've got a murder to plan, and I've got a suit to buy."

Chapter 6 - Carmen

I PUT MY coffee down on Nate's table. We'd regrouped in his rented apartment the next morning, Tuesday, seeing as I lived on-base. I couldn't exactly invite him to stay with me, because Captain P would lose his shit if he found out I was colluding with a foreign agent.

Dali sat at my side, and I scratched her head. The bathroom still smelled bad from yesterday, and while we were at the range, she'd chewed up a towel and one of Nate's favourite sneakers. Now he was barefoot, and every so often, he glared over at her and muttered something about South Koreans having the right idea. Well, he shouldn't have left his shoes in the bathroom, should he?

"We should buy her some toys," I said.

"No, we should buy her a bed. She spent all night trying to climb into mine."

Dammit, Carmen, don't get jealous of a dog.

"Okay, a bed and some toys. And a leash and a collar."

"Why don't we buy the whole pet store? Can we do some work now?"

Fine. Work. I gave Dali one last pat before I leaned forwards on my elbows.

"According to our sources, Lozano's retreated to his main compound on the edge of town and hired a dozen more ex-soldiers into the paramilitary group that provides his security."

"Two dozen," Nate said, glancing up from his laptop. "He also had to replace the ones who died in the explosion. Plus he's upgraded perimeter security to include extra cameras and motion detectors."

"How do you know that?"

"*My* sources."

"What sources?"

He just raised one annoying eyebrow.

"We're supposed to be working together."

"No, you're supposed to be coming up with a plan, and I'll help with the execution. That's what sidekicks do."

Yes, I understood the theory. The problem was, in all the plans anyone else came up with, I was always the one stuck half a mile away with a rifle, and I hadn't done much actual planning myself. While I'd done months and months of training in the military, there was a big difference between jungle warfare or anti-terror raids and the precision removal of one highly protected individual. Especially when I'd agreed to work with an arrogant American who'd spent the morning sulking because he didn't get his own way yesterday.

And worse, according to our researchers, Lozano had holed up behind a ten-foot-high wall topped with glass shards, and after the security breach at his weekend home, his security team was trigger-happy. A delivery driver had narrowly avoided losing his head when he couldn't locate the paperwork fast enough. Lozano hadn't been spotted outside since, and my gut said he'd stay safely in his reinforced bunker until the weekend. A near-death experience would be enough to rattle anyone, even a drug lord, and besides, he probably had to interview for *el antílope*'s replacement. How did one go about recruiting a man like that? Did potential applicants submit résumés?

Nate cleared his throat, still staring at me.

"Carmen?"

"The only event we're sure Lozano will attend in the near future is the Day of the Dead festival in town. His grandma organised the inaugural parade, and he sponsors the entire event. He hasn't missed one since it started."

I'd grown up thirty miles away, and the parade was famous throughout the region. People travelled for miles to watch. Last year, Lozano had presented the costume prizes, and the youngest winner burst into tears because she was scared of his mask. Me? I was more scared of the man behind it.

"And?" Nate asked. "What else?"

I settled into the chair behind my own laptop and opened the email that had just arrived.

"Lozano's due to arrive at twelve thirty as the floats go past the town hall, and he's got his own private viewing area above a restaurant he owns. A glassed-in balcony—bulletproof, unfortunately—and he's due to eat lunch there at one o'clock. Afterwards, he'll watch his niece perform a routine with her dance group."

"I'm aware of that."

"Is there anything you don't know?"

"Sure. Are we alone in the universe?" Nate started laughing as my palm itched to slap him.

"Can't you be serious for two minutes?"

His smile disappeared, and now he looked kind of

scary. Perhaps I preferred him being a dick.

"How do you plan to kill him?" he asked.

"I was thinking we could scout out locations around the restaurant for a medium-range shot as he exits. Somewhere with good line-of-sight and several escape routes."

"No way. Even if you did manage to get a bead on him without his guards getting in the way, there are too many civilians around."

"I'd use MagSafe ammunition. That wouldn't pass through when I hit him."

"And what happens when his bodyguards start firing back? You think they'd be so careful? That parade's gonna be full of kids."

"I can't get in close with a .22."

"You can't use a gun at all."

"Then what do you expect me to use? A knife?"

"No. Think outside the box."

Right. Because I had so much experience at that.

"I'm not sure how it works in America, but here they don't like us to get too creative. And our commanding officer sees us as expendable. You know the Special Forces motto? *Even death cannot stop us, and if death takes us by surprise, it's more than welcome.* If one of us dies because we screw up, there are twenty more hungry recruits waiting to take our place. Funerals and apologies are cheaper than training courses. Is this what you wanted? To sit there being all smug while you watch me fail?"

"I'll train you," he said softly.

"Huh?"

"You're not expendable, and if your commanding officer won't train you, then I will. Lie on the bed."

"What? No!"

Was this some kind of kinky game to him?

"Fine, then sit in the chair. But you need to relax, and then close your eyes."

"Why?"

"To think. You know the town, right? And you've done research on Lozano?"

"Yes."

"So remove any distractions and think through all the scenarios." He got up and headed to the sofa, where he made himself comfortable with his feet up. "Close your eyes, *querida*."

No way was I lying on his bed, but what about his other suggestion? None of the men I usually worked with wanted to see me succeed, but Nate's offer of help seemed genuine. I shut my eyes, propping my elbows on the table and resting my chin on my hands.

"Okay. What next?"

"Let's start off with listing all the ways a man can die."

"Shooting, stabbing, strangulation."

"Slow down. Begin by considering more general terms. Broadly speaking, most manners of death can be split into four categories: natural, accidental, homicide, and suicide. Forget natural for now because that's not why we're here. Focus on homicide, although we get bonus points if we can make it look like an accident or suicide. Then break it down further into causes of death, and we've got five of those. Mechanical, chemical, electrical, thermal, and asphyxia. Asphyxia's an interesting one, as it crosses over with the other four."

So clinical. Despite my chosen career path, a shiver

ran through me in the rented apartment, which now seemed far too cosy for its occupant.

"Okay, five ways to die."

"Exactly. Our job is to understand all the different ways to cause death, then select the most appropriate method for Señor Lozano. Tell me about thermal trauma first. How would you cause a body to overheat?"

"A fire? Explosives?"

"Those are the obvious answers, although in a fire, the subject is more likely to succumb to asphyxia first. Now think deeper. The temperature of the human body is thirty-seven degrees Celcius. We only need to push it out of that comfort zone to achieve our objective. How about trapping someone in a sauna? Or a meat locker? Or a truck on a hot day?"

"You've done that?"

"I'll neither confirm nor deny."

"Aren't you worried I might tell someone about this conversation?"

"No."

"No? Why not?"

"You know why."

I did. Not only would I end my career by admitting I'd been associating with Nate in this way, I'd also be signing my own death warrant. And Lozano would still be alive. Plus—and I hated to admit it—I kind of liked Nate. Even though he was clearly the master here, he didn't talk down to me the same way my colleagues did. One week before I was due back at work, and I could really learn something in that time.

Over the next three hours, Nate ran through the A to Z of assassination, and I did go and lie on his bed in the end because my head was spinning. Who knew there were so many ways to kill someone? Everything from radiation poisoning to a rapid, unplanned ascent while scuba diving that would explode a victim's lungs. *My* brain was in danger of suffering a haemorrhage by the time he sat up from his spot on the sofa.

"Need a coffee?" he asked.

"I need a new job. Maybe I'll retrain as an undertaker? Seems as though they'll have plenty of work with you around."

"Black or white? Sugar?"

"White, no sugar." I got up to join him, stretching from side to side to work out the kinks in my back. "But now we've gone through all that, what about Lozano? How does that help us?"

"Next, we do another exercise—run through everything we know about him and compare notes. His daily routine, his associates, locations he's likely to visit, his habits, anything that might help us. Tonight, you sleep on the discussion, and tomorrow, you mesh the target and the methodology together and come up with a plan."

"Me?"

"Have you forgotten that afternoon we spent at the range?"

I hadn't forgotten him taking his shirt off. Kind of wished I hadn't stopped him from tossing the pants too. Shit. I was in trouble here, and not just because of Lozano.

"Right. I'll come up with a plan."

Nate handed me a mug of coffee, too hot to drink, but I clutched it in front of me like a shield. Anything to keep him from getting closer. *Think, Carmen. Think.*

"Lozano's well known for his OCD," I said. "Every morning, he gets up at six o'clock exactly and spends an hour in the gym. Then his chef prepares breakfast, but he hates for anyone to watch him eat, so he always dines alone. Do you think we could poison his food?"

"According to my informant, somebody tastes every meal before he eats it, just in case. Lozano was paranoid even before the hit went wrong."

"You have an informant?"

"Not since Sunday."

"He died?"

"Unfortunately."

So Nate was in the dark. I still had my own intelligence resources to utilise, which perhaps gave me the upper hand, although I wasn't sure I wanted it anymore. Yesterday, my whole focus had been on winning, but if I'd taken the time to think straight, I'd have made sure to miss with every shot.

"Yes, that *is* unfortunate. My research says Lozano uses the mornings for meetings. Everyone comes to him. He used to travel a lot, but since he got caught up in an ambush six years ago, he prefers to stay at home."

"He lost part of the sight in his left eye afterwards," Nate said.

"That was never confirmed."

"Maybe not to you, but it happened."

How did he know so much?

"And he has a hygiene fetish," I said, eager to prove that I'd been thorough too. "Everything has to be spotless, he showers three times a day, and he wears gloves whenever he leaves his home."

"Agreed. He also refuses to set foot in public bathrooms and uses so much hand sanitiser he bought shares in the manufacturer of his favourite brand. He's actually invested well over the years. If he hadn't gone into the drug trade, he could have had a decent career on Wall Street."

"You sound as if you admire him. How can you?"

"I don't admire his ethics, just his business sense."

"He's a monster. They all are."

"And we'll kill him, but you need to focus and lose the emotion."

"Sorry. I..." A lump formed in my throat when I thought of Juliana, and I swallowed it back down. "Lozano has no wife, no girlfriend, no boyfriend. If he wants female company, he has a stable of women to call upon, but none ever stay the night."

"Hey, what's wrong?" The bed dipped as Nate sat beside me. "You sound all choked up."

"It's nothing."

"Bullshit."

I opened my eyes and found him looking at me, his expression a mix of nervousness and concern. Not something I'd ever expected to see from him.

"My sister died in the drug war, okay? It's why I joined the army. There was a shootout between two rival cartels, and she got caught in the crossfire."

"You wanted revenge?"

"Drugs—I don't care about them, or the money, but I want to stop more innocent people from getting hurt. I promise the past won't affect my work. I can squash the emotions away, compartmentalise, stop—"

Nate's hug surprised me, but it had been so long since anyone comforted me like that, and I just... It felt nice. Safe.

Dangerous.

I shoved him away.

"We're here to work. Nothing more, nothing less."

If I didn't know better, I'd have said the fleeting look in his eyes was hurt, but then I reminded myself that Nate was an asshole and he didn't do empathy.

"Then work, *querida*. Tell me about the chinks in Lozano's armour."

Right now, I was learning more about the chinks in my own, and I didn't like that feeling. Not one bit.

"These new guards—could they be vulnerable to bribery?"

"Possibly, but you have five days. We don't have time to find out."

"What about his family? Could we use them as leverage?"

"He's tightened security around them too."

"This is impossible."

"Not impossible, just difficult. Don't you like a challenge?"

Not anymore. Mostly, I was tired now. At twenty-three, I was ready to call it quits with this life, although I couldn't admit that to a man like Nate. A soft knock at the door saved me from having to answer, and my hand went automatically to the gun at my side. "Who's that? Are you expecting someone?"

"That'll be my clothes for this evening." He flashed me a grin, and heat rushed through me, settling in all the wrong places. "As your significant other, I figured I'd better impress your grandma."

Chapter 7 - Carmen

"PLEASE DON'T TALK," I said to Nate. "This evening will be bad enough already without getting a lecture from my family on my choice of man."

"What's wrong with me? I'm wearing a shirt and I promise I won't get drunk."

Two days ago, the list would have been endless—arrogant, rude, condescending, charmless, pushy, and so on, and so on—but now? I wasn't so sure.

"Just don't curse in front of my grandma. She hates that."

"No cursing. Understood."

He held out a hand to help me from the cab, and I ignored it, but I couldn't ignore the arm that slid around my waist. Dammit, I almost dropped my hastily cooked chicken tamale pie.

"What the hell are you doing? Get your hands off me!"

"*Querida*, we're supposed to be dating."

"Can't we date from a foot apart?"

"A man like me? That would never happen."

I took it all back. Nate was an egotistical jackass. A jackass with glutes of steel and a smile that made my heart go all bumpy. Dammit.

"Fine. Leave your arm where it is. But if your hand slides any lower, be prepared to lose fingers."

Dali skittered around at my feet, but Nate kept a tight grip on her leash. I wasn't sure she'd enjoy Grandma's party, but being shut in Nate's bathroom on her own wouldn't be much fun either. At least she'd get plenty of leftovers to fill out that skinny frame.

We'd only got halfway to the front door when it flew open. What the...? My brother ran out and did a double take at Nate and Dali before dragging us sideways behind the old jacaranda tree in the front garden. At least Dali had a proper collar and leash now—I'd visited the pet store after our earlier planning session— although Nate grumbled constantly about holding the puppy because her new accessories were pink.

"Teo, what are you doing?" I asked.

He ignored me in favour of looking Nate up and down, nodding to himself when he liked what he saw.

"Teodoro Hernandez. You're Carmen's new boyfriend?"

He said that like I'd had an old boyfriend when all I'd managed was a handful of mistakes. The longest had lasted two months, plus another three afterwards of ignoring his emails, gifts, and notes pledging his undying love.

"That's right. Nate Wood." They shook hands. "What's with the subterfuge?"

"The puppy's yours? I love the pink sparkles."

"We got it together."

Should I kill Nate now or later? A joint puppy implied a relationship, and we definitely didn't have one of those.

"Why are we hiding behind a tree?" I asked.

Teo focused on me, and I knew that look all too well. I'd first seen it aged six, when a four-year-old Teo confessed he'd cut my favourite doll's hair because Juliana, our older sister, told him it would grow back longer, only it didn't.

Whatever he had to say, I wouldn't like it.

"There's a small problem."

See?

"How small?"

"About this size." He held his thumb and forefinger about three quarters of an inch apart.

"Go on."

Please, don't let it be a disaster. I'd had enough of those already that week.

"I've been with Pasqual for almost a year now, and I love him. I really love him. So I bought him a promise ring."

"That's great." Of course it was—at least one of the Hernandez siblings had found happiness. "And you're gonna tell our parents? And Grandma? Is that what the difficulty is? Because you know I'll back you up."

"Not exactly. Grandma got cold and borrowed my jacket, and she found the ring in the inside pocket."

"So she knows already?"

"I couldn't tell her, Carmen. Not when she's only got a week left. I didn't want to upset her."

"That psychic was talking shit, you know that, yes?"

"What if she wasn't? Grandma's so convinced..."

Teo trailed off, and I began to get a bad, bad feeling.

"What did you tell her, then? About the ring?"

"I told her I was holding it for you. That you planned to propose to your boyfriend at the end of her birthday celebration."

"You did *what*?"

"I panicked." Teo backed away out of arm's reach,

rummaging in his pocket. "Here's the ring. All you have to do is pretend for a few days."

"A few days? Have you lost your mind?" I glanced at Nate, expecting him to be horrified, but instead he was trying not to laugh.

"We can fix it up next Tuesday when the deadline's passed. If Grandma dies, then she'll never find out, and if she doesn't die, I figure she'll be so happy it won't matter when you call the engagement off."

"You've really thought this through, haven't you?"

"It'll work; trust me. Besides, you owe us. Remember last year when that creep wouldn't stop sending those pleading messages and Pasqual pretended to be your boyfriend for two whole weeks?"

"What creep?" Nate asked.

"It doesn't matter. He's gone now. Teo, there's a difference between this and what Pasqual did. He was a willing participant."

"Grandma's been complaining of chest pains, but since she found out about the proposal, it's given her a new lease of life. She's even ordered an extra cake."

"We're not the only people involved. Have you forgotten Nate? Because he's standing right here."

"He's crazy about you. I can tell just by looking."

Teo was the crazy one if he thought that. But when I glanced at Nate, he shrugged.

"It's for less than a week, right?"

"You can't seriously be considering going along with this?"

"Why not? It'll be worth it to see you on your knees in front of me."

That pig. "I hate both of you."

Nate's arm tightened around my waist, and his

hand slid down an inch. I shot him a warning glare, but he ignored it.

"Think of your grandma, *querida*. She'd want to see you happy before she passes." He let go and pantomimed a look of shock, mouth open and one hand on each cheek. "What do you think? Convincing enough?"

"Raise your eyebrows a little more and it'll be perfect," Teo said.

"This is the worst idea you've ever had," I told my brother. "And considering you once brought a baby coral snake home in your glasses case, that's a real achievement."

Now Nate's eyebrows rose. "You really did that?"

"I was eight years old and I liked the colours."

"He wanted to keep it as a pet," I added.

"Snake or no snake, you need to do this for Grandma." Teo held the promise ring out. "Here you go."

I took it from him like it was poisonous. A plain silver band, engraved on the inside with the words *I'll always be yours*. Ugh. I never wanted to belong to a man, and definitely not one as bossy as Nate.

"Bro, I'm gonna add one condition," my fake fiancé-to-be said, and I screwed my eyes shut. Fiancé-to-be? I'd somehow walked through the portal to hell.

"Anything. A romantic meal? A honeymoon?"

"We've got a busy week, so the puppy's yours until Monday."

"Ooh, deal! Pasqual loves dogs, and so do I."

The front door opened behind us again, and this time, it was my mamá.

"Carmen? Why are you still outside? The drinks are

getting warm, and Aunt Teresa's brought her home-made guacamole."

Nate's hand came back, an inch lower than before, and I gritted my teeth rather than make a scene.

"Just coming, Mamá."

"No more tequila, *querida*."

Nate took the glass from me. I tried half-heartedly to get it back, but he held it out of reach.

"I need it."

"If you drink any more, you won't be able to ask your little question later."

"Which is the exact reason I'm drinking."

He put the glass on the nearest table and leaned down to kiss my hair. Nate was far better at this charade than me, and I'd given up trying to fight it. His other hand now rested firmly on my ass cheek, and I sagged against him as I watched Grandma from across the room. She kept sneaking not-so-subtle glances in our direction, and every time she caught my eye, she smiled. How could I ruin her dream? I may not be able to get married before she left us, but the least I could do was pretend to be engaged.

The party she'd spent months organising was a bizarre cross between a birthday celebration and a living wake, with plenty of Día de los Muertos references thrown in for good measure. Pictures of my whole family scrolled past on a light projector, sugar skulls jostled for space between balloons and piñatas, and someone had put a book of condolence on one end of the buffet table. What kind of man would want to marry into this insanity for real?

Pasqual arrived, and Teo had obviously filled him in on the deception because he gave my shoulders a squeeze.

"Thanks for doing this. I'll organise the flowers for your wedding, free of charge."

Pasqual owned a florist, the biggest one in town, and over the last year, his floral arrangements had grown popular among celebrities. He was talking about opening more branches, but I could lighten his load a little.

"We're only pretending to be engaged to save your ass," I hissed.

He looked sideways at Nate. "*Si*, of course. I mean when you eventually do get married."

Why bother wasting my breath? Words were becoming more difficult now, as was standing up, and I just wanted to get the whole stupid, embarrassing proposal over with. Someone behind me tapped a glass with a knife, and I jumped and stumbled, but Nate kept me on my feet.

"Looks as if your grandma wants to make a speech."

Maravilloso, just when I thought things couldn't get any worse.

"I'd like to thank you all for coming today," she started, beaming at everyone in the room and looking remarkably healthy for a lady with five days to live. "After my Francisco passed, I thought my heart would never heal, but it was then that I learned the true meaning of friends and family, and to have you here celebrating the little time I have left makes the chest of an old lady swell with joy..."

The ring burned against my palm, a tiny torture

device waiting to unleash its full force. Could I really go through with this? Perhaps I could pretend there was an emergency at work? A shortage of beef or a quality-control issue with tortillas. Or I could leap into my car, drive to the airport, and get on the nearest plane. At least, I could if I hadn't been drinking. Right now, I'd probably crash into the lamp post fifty yards down the road. Plus there was a small technical glitch in that my car was still parked outside Nate's apartment.

Oh, hell. The whole room had fallen silent, and worse, Grandma was staring at me expectantly. This was the moment, wasn't it?

"You okay?" Nate mouthed.

No, but I dropped to my knees anyway, which put me at eye level with the not-insignificant bulge of Nate's crotch. I licked my lips in an unconscious gesture then realised what I'd done. The horror! Nate had noticed too, and that grin was back.

Fuck, I just needed to get this over with so I could die quietly of shame somewhere. Only Grandma's look of rapture made me carry on.

"Nate, I realise this is crazy, but I *am* crazy, so I guess it fits, and from the moment this idea was planted in my head, it's grown and grown and now it's huge..." *Don't look at his cock, Carmen.* "But I need to ask you because I know how much it means to Grandma, and how much you mean to me, and..." *Stop waffling.* "Will you marry me?"

"Of course I will, *querida*."

He hauled me to my feet, and I found myself plastered against him, which was a good thing and a bad thing. Good because my knees would have buckled otherwise, and also he felt warm and strong and kind of comfortable. And very, very bad because Grandma was hopping around like a madwoman and now she had a freaking camera.

"Kiss each other! We need pictures! You two make such an adorable couple."

Kiss him? No, I definitely hadn't thought this one through, had I?

Only Nate's lips were coming towards mine, all soft and smoochy, and his tongue too. Okay, that actually felt nice. Cheers erupted as I kissed him back, but then I came to my senses and so did my stomach.

"Let me go!"

I tried to push him away, but there were people everywhere and I couldn't move or swallow or breathe.

"I'm gonna be sick," I mumbled.

Then I was in Nate's arms, in the hallway, in the bathroom, and he held my hair back as I vomited a month's worth of tequila into the toilet. Well, wasn't that the perfect metaphor for my fucked-up life?

Where was my damn gun?

CHAPTER 8 - NATE

CARMEN STIRRED IN Nate's arms, and he started a mental countdown.

Ten... Nine... Eight... Seven...

"What the hell are you doing? Get off!"

"*Querida*, you're the one who's lying on top of me." On the floor. In her parents' house.

She rolled away, which only made things worse.

"Where are my pants?" she screeched.

"Shh, or you'll wake the whole house."

The death glare was so much better.

"Where. Are. My. Fucking. Pants?"

"In the laundry hamper along with your shirt. Don't you remember anything that happened last night?"

Now she fell silent. Silent and a little worried, judging by the way she bit her bottom lip. Her hands shook as she lifted the sheet he'd covered himself with, the sheet she'd wormed her way underneath in the middle of the night, totally unaware of what she was doing. He'd kept his shirt and pants on, and somehow got her and her spaghetti arms into a clean T-shirt, but she still couldn't meet his gaze.

"We didn't, did we?"

"Didn't what?"

"Didn't... You really want me to spell it out?"

"I think so, yes."

There was something incredibly hot about her when she got all flustered and angry, and the devil in Nate just couldn't help winding her up.

Carmen covered her eyes with her hands, then gritted her teeth and whacked him with a pillow.

"Well, I'm not going to. You know exactly what I'm talking about."

"Would it have been such a terrible thing?"

Silence. Nate figured that was better than an outright no.

"Nothing happened, okay?" He decided to put her out of her misery. "I tried to put you to bed, but you insisted that I was the guest and you'd sleep on the floor. Three times, I moved you, and three times, you grabbed the spare blanket and threw yourself down in front of the window. In the end, I gave up, so we both slept here." Nate allowed himself a smile. "Can't say I minded."

Carmen closed her eyes again and groaned. "I threw up, didn't I?"

"So you didn't forget everything."

"I'm so sorry. I just got nervous, and I didn't realise how much I was drinking, and..."

Nate pressed a finger to her lips.

"It's okay. It doesn't matter."

"It does. Who proposes to the man she supposedly loves, then vomits on him?"

"If it helps, you only got my shoes."

She burrowed under the covers, curling herself up in a tiny ball. Fuck. The woman was certifiable, but Nate's inner caveman didn't seem to care about that. He realised at that moment that when he got on a plane back to Virginia, he wanted her beside him, every last kooky atom in her.

"Carmen?"

"This is all a nightmare. I'll wake up soon."

Nate got to his knees and lifted her into the same position, facing him. She was fit, but although Carmen was an inch or two taller than Emmy, she didn't have the same bulk that Black's protégé had packed on over the last year. Or the same obstreperous attitude, thank fuck.

"You can't go back to sleep." Nate brushed a few strands of dark hair out of her face and tucked them behind her ear. "We need to deal with Lozano."

"My head hurts."

Carmen's shirt had ridden up, and it was all Nate could do to drag his gaze away from the dark triangle showing through her panties and direct it up to her face. The woman wore delicate underwear made from lace, and last night, he'd gone to sleep so hard it was painful. At least Mrs. Hernandez hadn't made good on her promise to check in on them both later.

"Do you want me to take care of everything? I'll need your help with one or two things, but I've got a plan."

"A plan? You've got a plan? What plan?"

"You don't need to worry about that yet. Shall I take over?"

Conflicting emotions warred in Carmen's eyes. She'd fought so hard to keep control, to win the shooting match and prove her abilities, but inside, she knew she was out of her depth. The question was, would she concede to Nate?

Finally, she slumped forwards. "Okay. Please."

Thank goodness. Missing that fucking dime was the

best move Nate had ever made.

"And we'll see you both soon? Sunday, for my final goodbye?"

Nate bent to give Grandma Hernandez a kiss on her leathery cheek. The old woman was batshit crazy with all her talk of death—she'd even chosen her own casket, walnut with a cream satin lining—but Nate still liked her. In fact, he liked the whole family and their closeness. Probably because his family had been the total opposite—his parents had divorced before he could talk; his mom was more interested in the twins, his half-sisters by her new husband; and Nate didn't even know where his biological father was. Nor did he particularly care.

Being suddenly thrust into the middle of a new family was weird, but happy weird. And Carmen's mom made great huevos rancheros. He'd eaten Carmen's plateful too seeing as she wasn't all that hungry.

"Sure, we'll be here Sunday."

Carmen muttered something that sounded like "kill me now," but she nodded anyway.

Grandma was still holding onto Nate's biceps. "I'm so happy Carmen's found herself a nice young man."

He ignored Carmen's eye-roll. "It's been a pleasure to meet her wonderful family. Do you want us to bring anything at the weekend?"

"Just yourselves. We'll arrange everything else, don't you worry."

Nate didn't worry. That afternoon, he was more concerned with getting Carmen back to bed and making the final arrangements for Lozano's death. She didn't look so good. Slightly green around the edges.

Back at the apartment, he scooped her out of the cab and carried her upstairs along with her travel bag. She'd packed a few essentials before she left, and secretly, Nate was damn happy she planned on staying with him, although he couldn't let it show and risk scaring her off.

While Carmen slept peacefully in his bed, he set up his laptop and hacked into Lozano's emails again. Without an informant, that was the best source of information Nate had left. Nothing had changed. Lozano would still be attending the Día de los Muertos parade on Saturday, and his costume was due to be delivered on the same morning, three hours before his scheduled lunch. Lozano had been using the same designer for years, an elegant woman named Verónica Camacho who specialised in the flamboyant designs worn in carnivals the world over. Since her studio was so near to Lozano's home, she measured him personally and remained available for any alterations.

Nate had been intercepting Verónica's emails too, and her phone calls, going back weeks on the off chance that a backup plan would be needed. He'd also passed some of those recordings to Yolanda, an old friend at the CIA and a Spanish speaker who'd impersonate anyone for a bottle of Patrón.

He fired off a quick email, asking her to stand by on Saturday, ready for the phone call Lozano was sure to make.

Finally, he headed to the bathroom and took a shower. Did he look better with stubble or without? His research said Verónica hadn't been in a serious relationship for years, but when she dated, she preferred younger men a little on the rough side. He didn't bother to shave.

After he'd added contacts to lighten his eyes and a squirt of aftershave, he shook the bottle labelled "shaving oil" that sat so innocently beside the sink. An acquaintance had passed it to him back in Virginia—another assassin—and no, he didn't ask how the hell she'd managed to obtain the stuff. From what he knew about her, he suspected she'd made it herself, and the idea of the bitch cooking up nerve agents in her kitchen scared the shit out of him.

On the two occasions she'd invited him over for dinner, he'd politely declined.

Black, of course, had gone and lived to tell the tale.

Now, Nate headed back to the sleeping area and knelt beside the bed. Carmen stirred as he trailed the backs of his fingers down her cheek, and this time, she didn't shout at him when she woke up. See? They were making progress.

"I have to go out, *querida*."

"What? Why?"

"I'll explain later. Just get some sleep, and I'll be back to take you for dinner."

"What about Lozano?"

"Don't worry about Lozano."

Nate kissed her on the forehead, and when she gave a soft sigh, he almost said fuck the job, fuck Lozano, and stayed with her. But he couldn't. Not just for his sake, but for hers. She was counting on him to pull this off.

The last thing he did before he left the apartment was remove the ring she'd put on his finger last night, the ring he already felt entirely too comfortable wearing. Instead, he slipped it into her hand and pressed his lips to her knuckles.

"Take care of this, okay?"

She gripped it tight and nodded. "Nate?"

"Yeah?"

"Thank you."

CHAPTER 9 - CARMEN

WHERE WAS NATE? He said he'd be back in time for dinner, but it was half past eight and the apartment was silent. Was he okay? I'd got his phone number from Captain P's secretary, but when I tried calling, it went straight to voicemail.

I'd already searched his apartment out of curiosity —the man used more beauty products than I did—and now I was starting to get worried. Logic told me a man like Nate could look after himself, and even if he had gotten into trouble, it shouldn't have mattered because I didn't like him anyway.

My fingers went to my forehead again, to the spot where he'd kissed me before he left. No, I absolutely didn't like him.

Well, maybe just a little, but not in *that* way.

More in the way that a girl respected a colleague, except I didn't respect many of mine. The last guy I'd gotten on okay with other than Nestor, a seven-year veteran of GAFE who'd had the decency to address my face rather than my chest when he spoke, had recently been jailed for colluding with one of Lozano's competitors.

Perhaps I should stop being so ambitious and accept that I was better off shooting people from a distance? Every time I tried talking, I just got myself into trouble.

Like now. Here I was, stuck in the apartment of a man I barely knew, waiting for him to help me fix up my mess. After all, the short deadline was mine, not his. If I weren't involved, he could take a step back and regroup, then make a proper plan rather than rushing in with something half-formed. What if he didn't come back? How would I let his family know? Did he even have a family? Should I start calling the hospitals?

The lock clicked.

Training meant I had my gun in my hand before the door swung open, but I quickly lowered it when I saw it was Nate.

"Are you okay?"

"Why wouldn't I be?"

"Because you went out alone to do a dangerous job?" He got closer, and I took in his appearance. The untucked shirt. The undone buttons. The red smear on his face. "Is that lipstick on your cheek?"

"Probably."

"*Probably*? Is that all you've got to say?"

He smelled of alcohol too, although he still seemed perfectly coherent.

"Jealous, *querida*?"

"What? No! Of course not."

The asshole didn't answer, just sauntered away and dropped his jacket onto the bed. I almost stormed off, but then he started undoing the rest of his buttons and my feet refused to move. Instead, I stood there with my hands on my hips, desperately trying to think of something smart to say.

Nate balled the shirt up and tossed it through the bathroom door, straight into the laundry hamper.

"You sure about that?" he asked.

"I'm just angry that we've got a job to do and a deadline to meet, and you disappeared off on a date. I had no idea whether you were alive or dead since you didn't answer your phone."

"I turned it off to avoid interruptions, but it's nice to know you care."

That... That... "I care about my career."

"Rumour has it your new captain's on Pablo Huerta's payroll. Did you know that?"

Pablo Huerta was one of Lozano's main rivals. "Where did you hear that? What evidence is there?"

"Just a whisper or two right now, nothing concrete. But that doesn't mean the rumours are wrong."

No, it didn't. And it wouldn't be the first time members of GAFE had betrayed our country for the opposition either. In 1999, a good number of elite operatives joined Osiel Cárdenas Guillén to form the Los Zetas cartel, and years of bloodshed followed.

"Fine. I don't enjoy my job. Happy? But I believe in our objective, which is to rid Mexico of as many Lozanos and Huertas and Guilléns as we can."

"You can do that without working for GAFE."

"How? I couldn't even come up with a plan for Lozano on my own."

"You've got a month left in the army?"

"Nice to see you've been through my personnel records."

"I heard you talking to your mom about it last night."

Oh. Oops. "Yes, I've got a month left, but I'll probably sign up for another year at least."

"Why don't you try working somewhere else?"

"Because I don't want to work for a criminal, and in case you haven't noticed, there aren't many legitimate opportunities for snipers around here."

"You could move away. To another country, even."

"My family's in Mexico."

Mexico's Special Forces Corps was based in Temamatla, not far from where I grew up on the outskirts of Mexico City. I went home every time I had a day off, and Mamá still did half of my laundry. Sure, it felt suffocating at times, but could I really move to a whole other country? The only foreigner I knew was Nate, and I wasn't even sure if I liked him most of the time. But on the other hand, did I want to spend another year of my life at GAFE, dreading every new set of orders I received?

"Yes, I know that," Nate said. "It would be a big move if you decided to leave."

"I'll think about it."

"I wouldn't expect you to do anything else. Come on, let's get dinner, and I'll explain what I was doing tonight. That burrito place on the corner any good?"

"There's a better one three streets away."

Nate tugged on a T-shirt and held out a hand. I stared at it.

"If we're getting married, you should at least be able to hold hands."

"We're not getting married."

"Your grandma seemed convinced we were."

"The pair of you deserve each other."

"She's a bit old for me, don't you think? Plus that satin-lined casket she's ordered might be slightly small for two."

"You're still wearing lipstick."

"Shit." He grabbed a tissue and scrubbed at his face. "Gone?"

It was. And when he smiled at me, I wanted the other woman, whoever she was, to be gone as well.

And then when I took his hand, it didn't feel awkward like I'd feared. No, it felt entirely too normal, and that was what scared me.

CHAPTER 10 - CARMEN

NATE LED ME into the restaurant, and Pedro behind the counter stared unblinking as we walked all the way to the back. Nate scowled as he pulled out a chair for me.

"Hasn't that *cabrón* ever seen a pretty girl before?"

I didn't know whether to be pleased that Nate thought I was pretty or pissed because he'd insulted a friend of mine. In the end, I went with both. As a woman, I was perfectly capable of multitasking.

"I've known Pedro since school. He's most likely surprised because I'm with a man who isn't my brother."

The creep, Antonio, had always refused to eat in my favourite little hole-in-the-wall joints, favouring expensive restaurants instead. My fault for dating a businessman who owned a fancy imported BMW, I'd soon realised. He always thought he was better than everyone else—that and being clingy were just two of his many, many faults.

"Now who's acting jealous?" I asked.

Nate didn't bother to answer, just shuffled over a little on the bench seat so our legs touched.

"Pedro's been married to his high school sweetheart for two years. I went to their wedding."

"Good. I'm happy for them."

"What car do you drive?" I asked Nate.

"A Porsche. Why?"

Shit.

"No reason."

"There's always a reason."

"I don't like men who drive expensive cars."

"You wouldn't like me if I drove a fifteen-year-old Honda."

I had to laugh. "True."

"What did he do to you?"

"Who?"

"Expensive-car-dude."

"How do you know it was one person in particular? Maybe I just hate capitalists."

"What if I'm just a regular guy who won the lotto?"

"And bought a really expensive gun?"

"Says the woman shooting the AWM."

"Expensive-car-dude gave me a diamond bracelet. I sold it to buy the AWM." Nate was looking at me funny. Well, kind of past me, into the distance, except there wasn't any distance because there was a wall there. "Why are you staring like that?"

"No reason."

"There's always a reason."

"True. And I'll tell you one day, but not right now." He gave his head a little shake. "We need to go over our schedule for the rest of the week."

"The mysterious 'plan,' yes?" I used my fingers to make little quote marks around the word. "Should we be discussing that here?"

"As long as we keep our voices down, it's probably safer than anywhere else. Harder to bug a restaurant."

"You think the apartment's bugged?"

"No, but why take the chance? How about you order us what's good, and we can get started?"

Ten minutes later, Pedro had served up corn tacos filled with refried beans, carne asada, and a topping of cheese. Not something I ate every day, but delicious when I didn't want to cook. Or when I was with Nate, whose rented kitchen held only protein shakes, coffee, milk, half a bag of flour left over from the chicken tamale pie I'd made there, and a single can of beer.

But there was no beer tonight, not when we needed to concentrate on plotting.

"Come closer," Nate said as he pulled my chair towards him and tucked his arm around my shoulders.

I couldn't even be mad, because there was an unseasonable chill in the air tonight and he was warm. Hot, even. I leaned into him, and to all the world, we must have looked like two lovers having a deep and meaningful conversation rather than a pair of warring assassins discussing murder.

"So," I asked. "Which of us is doing the deed? Who's going to get up close to Lozano and pull the trigger?"

He smiled, not his usual arrogant grin, but a cunning curve of his lips that sent a shiver through me.

"Neither of us."

"Neither of us? How is that possible?"

"Lozano's going to do it himself. How much do you know about binary poisons?"

"A poison? But we already discussed that—he won't eat food until a minion's tried it first, and we'd never get close enough to inject it."

"We don't have to."

"What are you going to do? Spray it from a

distance? Someone else might get in the way."

"Anything's possible, but it's unlikely. Binary poisons work in two parts, and until they're put together, they won't do any damage. And even combined, it'll dissipate before anyone who matters gets close. At worst, we'll damage a few of his henchmen, which is no bad thing."

"I guess. But that still doesn't answer the question of how we get it near Lozano."

"Tonight, I was out with the lady who's making Lozano's costume for the Day of the Dead parade. Verónica Camacho. She's due to deliver it on Saturday morning, except you're gonna take it instead, along with the first chemical agent."

"How? I don't even know her."

"Because I'll keep her occupied."

"You're going to kidnap her? But she hasn't done anything wrong. What if—" Then it hit me. Literally, like a punch to the stomach. Nate's tequila breath. The lipstick on his face. "You plan to fuck her?"

"I wouldn't put it quite so crudely. I plan to keep her entertained."

"All through Friday night and into Saturday?"

"Better to start sooner to allow for any hiccups."

Now my stomach dropped into my shoes, although I didn't know why. Okay, I did. I just didn't want to admit it. I liked Nate. Despite him being bossy and a know-it-all and generally annoying, he lit me up from the inside out with an intoxicating fire of anger and lust.

I didn't want him to fuck Verónica because I wanted him to fuck me.

"What happens if you're not her type? Kidnapping

her would be safer."

"Trust me, I'm her type. She was all over me this evening."

I felt sick. "She might come to her senses."

"You forget my natural charm." He leaned in, his lips brushing against my ear. "I can be very persuasive when I want to be."

Charm? No, that wasn't it. The man leached testosterone through every pore, mixed with a healthy dose of pheromones and the occasional innuendo. That little spot between my legs pulsed, and I squirmed in my seat.

"What about the poison? What are we using?" I asked in a desperate attempt to change the subject.

When he told me, I almost wished he hadn't. On that quiet Wednesday evening, I realised just how fucked in the head Nate was. Only a genius would have come up with that plan. A genius or a madman.

And still I wanted him.

CHAPTER 11 - NATE

VERÓNICA CAMACHO STOOD the same height as Nate in her ridiculously tall shoes, and he suspected she'd only worn them so she had an excuse to keep clutching at his arm. She had to be a decade older, but she'd looked after herself, and she didn't need to wear all the make-up she'd troweled on—layers of black mascara, powder caking her face, and that scarlet lipstick she liked to leave all over him as though she was staking a claim.

Too bad he'd already set his sights on another woman.

"Another drink, Carlos?"

Just for fun, Nate had borrowed Black's first name, the name he hated and never used, and put a Spanish twist on it.

"One more and I have to get back to my hotel for that conference call, but let me buy them. Same again?"

She nodded and smiled, still perfectly poised. It would be a different story tomorrow night, when he planned to convince her to switch from palomas, the tame little grapefruit-flavoured cocktails she seemed so fond of, to straight tequila or mezcal. When he'd first visited her shop yesterday to buy a costume for the Día de los Muertos themed party he planned to attend in Mexico City tomorrow, she'd eagerly accepted his invitation to join him, and this evening, she'd made it clear what she hoped to get out of the arrangement. The hand on his crotch was a dead giveaway.

In the past, that wouldn't have been a problem, more a perk of the job. A reward for his hard work. But with Carmen back at the apartment, sleeping in his bed —even if he wasn't sleeping in it with her—he had to find a way to avoid any entanglement with the middle-aged Barbie doll.

He'd spent some more time at the shop today, being charming in a way Carmen wouldn't believe as well as checking out Lozano's costume and getting a look at the order book. That confirmed what he'd seen in Lozano's emails—Verónica was due to deliver the outfit at ten o'clock on Saturday. No sooner, no later.

Except Verónica would be passed out in the bedroom if Nate had anything to do with it.

Now, she sipped daintily on the paloma Nate had just bought and introduced him to another equally artificial friend, one who seemed determined to get her money's worth out of the breasts she'd undoubtedly paid a fortune for by thrusting them into the face of any man who walked past.

"Are you going to the parade on Saturday, Carlos?" she asked.

"Isn't everyone? I hear it's to die for."

Her high-pitched giggle made Nate's ears hurt. "I'm having a party on Sunday night. Do you both want to come?"

Verónica nodded without even consulting him. "What time does it start?"

"Eight o'clock. Luis will be playing with his band." The friend glanced at Nate and lowered her voice. "But it's okay, he got a new guitarist."

Another of Verónica's conquests? Nate got the impression she'd had a few, but he didn't care. If everything went according to plan, he'd be on a plane when the party began, flying somewhere far, far away.

And if karma looked kindly upon him after what he did to Lozano, Carmen would be at his side.

When Nate crept into his temporary home just before midnight, he found the table set for one with a note between the cutlery.

I didn't know if you'd eat, so I left food in the fridge. Microwave it for three minutes if you're hungry.

Carmen had bought him dinner? No, not bought it, he found when he peeped under the plate she'd placed over an earthenware dish. She'd fucking *made* him dinner. And he'd wasted the entire evening with a pair of vapid socialites.

Shit.

He tiptoed over to the bed, where she was breathing softly and evenly, that curtain of dark hair spread over his pillow. Nate almost crawled in beside her, but he was only twenty-seven and he didn't want to die so young. Instead, he bent to place a soft kiss on her forehead.

"Sweet dreams, *querida*."

For once, he slept well too. Usually, he dreamed of death, of the horrors he'd seen over the past decade in various wars and operations that only Black and a handful of others knew about. But tonight was different. Tonight, he dreamed of the woman he'd fallen in sudden, terrifying, messy love with.

Chapter 12 - Carmen

NATE WALKED OUT of the bathroom wearing only a towel, and I didn't know where to look. Well, I did, but it wouldn't have been appropriate, and nor would licking away that single drop of water running down his solid chest. Last night, I'd had this weird dream that he'd come home and kissed me, and now I couldn't think straight.

"Let's go over the plan one more time," he said.

"Sure."

The drop of water had reached his abs now, leaving a shiny trail behind it. How long did he spend in the gym? Muscles like that didn't happen overnight, and—

"Carmen? You okay?"

"Perfect," I snapped. All I had to do was facilitate a man's death while Nate had sex with a leggy brunette. I'd never met Verónica Camacho, but I'd looked her up on the internet and I hated her already. "Never better."

He paused halfway through buttoning up his dress shirt. "I know this isn't how you usually work, and I get that you're nervous, but it's the best option right now. Lozano's security is at an all-time high."

"I'm not nervous."

Not about the job, anyway. How hard could it be to deliver a costume? What worried me was the aftermath. If Lozano died, Nate would return to

Virginia, and my decision over my future would be a step closer. Should I stay here in Mexico with my family, working for a man I hated, or take a huge risk and quit?

If I left the army, I'd have two choices—get a normal job, one where I didn't have to shoot people, or move further afield and keep my guns. Last time I'd considered that, the only people hiring had been private security companies looking for contractors to work overseas in the Middle East and Africa. I'd never even left Latin America before.

"Everyone gets nervous, *querida*. It's nothing to be ashamed of. Turn around."

"What?"

"Turn around. I'm about to drop the towel, and I don't want you screaming harassment."

Seeing him naked, I'd be screaming something else, but I could hardly admit to that. I turned around, but thankfully I could still see his reflection in the glass of the kitchen cabinets. Holy fuck. The man was hung like a donkey. Heat flashed through me as he slowly pulled on a pair of boxer briefs and adjusted himself, and I bit my tongue—hard—to stop myself from groaning as he put on a pair of flannel pants that hugged his ass.

"I don't make complaints over *little* things like that."

It was true; I didn't. More than one of my colleagues had let it all hang loose in front of me, some because they were perverts and some because they were trying to shock me, but I'd mastered my poker face. Letting them know they'd gotten to me would only have made the problem worse.

Nate just chuckled. "There's nothing little about

me, *querida*. Okay, it's safe now." Once I'd turned back, he motioned me over. "All you have to do is drop the costume off and leave. Nothing more. If anything makes you feel uncomfortable, abort, and we'll come up with a new plan."

"Not before Monday, we won't."

"Your commanding officer's an asshole. Sometimes these things take longer, and he'll have to accept that."

"He won't."

"As I said before, there are other jobs out there."

"For a man like you, maybe."

"And a woman like you. Your skill set is unique."

"Well, if you hear of anyone looking for a twenty-three-year-old sniper with a moral code and a strong dislike of male chauvinist pigs, feel free to let me know."

Nate flashed me a grin. "I might just do that."

"I'm being serious."

"So am I." His smile faded, and he squeezed my hand. "I'm very serious, Carmen. Don't do anything risky today. Taking an extra month to deal with Lozano isn't a problem. You getting hurt? That's a big problem. Promise me."

"I won't take any risks."

"Promise me and mean it."

Aaaaaand he was back to being pushy. "I've been in GAFE High Command for over a year. I *am* trained to kill people, you know."

He stepped closer, only three inches away now. "Mean it."

"Fine." I crossed my fingers behind my back. "I promise I won't take any risks."

"Better." He fished around in his pocket and came

up with a brooch, a multicoloured sugar skull complete with flowers and a malevolent grin. "I got this for you."

A gift? He'd bought me a gift? "Cute."

"It's got a transmitter built into the back. Make sure you wear it when you go to visit Lozano so I can hear what's going on."

Not so cute. "You don't trust me?"

"I worry about you."

"I keep telling you—"

"Yes, I know, but I'm not going to stop worrying." He leaned down to kiss me on the forehead, just like in my dream, and my knees went weak. "Time for me to go, *querida*. See you tomorrow."

Chapter 13 - Nate

NATE SMILED TO himself as he listened through a hidden earpiece. Carmen obviously hadn't realised the brooch was transmitting already, because she was singing softly to herself as she moved around his apartment.

Unfortunately, Verónica assumed the smile was meant for her and took the opportunity to flick open one of his buttons and slide her hand inside his shirt. Nine o'clock, she was still only halfway drunk, and she'd already made noises about retiring back to her place. Heading to the apartment over the costume shop had always been part of Nate's plan, but not while Verónica was still conscious.

He turned to the barman. "Got a bottle of Asombroso Añejo?"

"Of course."

Beside Nate, Verónica giggled with delight. He'd quickly learned that she placed a lot of importance on both appearances and money, so she'd be sure to drink a two-hundred-dollar bottle of tequila. The barman poured them both shots—Nate's second drink of the night and Verónica's sixth—and Nate clinked his glass against hers.

"Here's to tonight, to great music and the company of a beautiful woman."

"Here's to getting naked."

Fucking great. At least she'd started slurring slightly. When he'd spoken to Black earlier, predictably his so-called friend had found the situation all too amusing. Not that he'd told Black about his feelings for Carmen—he still didn't understand those himself. And Black's pearl of wisdom? *Be prepared, buddy. Remember Kaitlyn Swanson.*

Like Nate would ever forget that night. Bruce Swanson, a fifty-five-year-old accountant with a penchant for the finer things in life, had managed the finances of a particularly dirty politician, one long suspected of accepting foreign bribes while remaining squeaky clean on the surface. On a viciously cold Friday evening two years previously, when Bruce and his wife were on a weekend break in Aspen, Black had come up with the bright idea of enlisting Kaitlyn's help to get into her father's home, a three-storey Victorian he'd turned into a homage to Fort Knox.

All Black needed to do was get friendly with Kaitlyn then take a look around when she fell asleep. Simple, right? It should have been, but Kaitlyn had a sorority sister with her, so Nate got enlisted to play wingman. Then the two girls decided they wanted a four-way, and they'd been fucking insatiable. In the end, Black had given both of them a taste of GHB before the two men died of exhaustion. On the bright side, Black had cleaned up the mess of champagne and condoms in the bedroom while Nate hacked into Swanson's computer and found what they were looking for.

With that in mind, when midnight hit, Nate slipped a roofie into Verónica's final shot of tequila. She'd already tried to drag him into the bar's bathroom with her, and there was no way she'd behave on the car ride home otherwise.

Problem solved.

Or so he thought at first. Verónica's driver gave Nate a sympathetic look as he carried her out of the car back at the shop.

"Did Señorita Camacho drink too much again?"

Nate grimaced. "I couldn't stop her. She do this often?"

"About every other week, although usually she can still walk. Want me to get the door for you?"

"Thanks, buddy."

With Verónica safely snoring in bed, still fully clothed apart from her shoes, Nate settled onto the sofa in her room to keep an eye on her vitals. Having her choke on her own vomit would throw an unnecessary wrench into the works.

Then he heard it.

Or rather, her.

A soft gasp in his ear, followed by a quiet whimper. *Carmen.* What the hell was she doing? She didn't sound distressed, more... No way. Was she even awake? The breathy little moans continued, and Nate's dick turned to rock, but he didn't dare take care of himself, not with Verónica tossing and turning so close by. No, he was reduced to listening, an aural voyeur if you like, until Carmen let out a long exhale followed by three whispered words. *I hate you.*

Fuck. Who did she hate? After what he imagined she'd been doing, it had to be a man, didn't it?

What if she'd been talking about him?

Morning came with Verónica still sleeping soundly. Nate had tried to grab a couple of hours' shut-eye, but the soundtrack of Carmen getting herself off played over and over in his head, and by the time the sun rose, he'd been awake for the entire night. Coffee. He needed coffee. While he was in the kitchen, he dug out a jug of water and headache pills for Sleeping Beauty upstairs, because she'd surely need them when she finally woke up.

Which happened at eight thirty when Carmen rang the bell downstairs, right on time.

"Who is it?" Verónica groaned.

"I'll go and find out. Just sleep, sweetheart."

"What happened last night?"

"The tequila hit you a little hard."

She looked at her arms and realised she was still in her sparkly dress, jewellery and all.

"Did we...?"

Nate forced a smile. "You blew my mind, baby. Don't you remember what happened in the bathroom at the bar?" A few locks of hair flopped across her face as she tried to sit up, and he brushed them to the side. "Are you okay? You look sick."

With those words, she clutched at her stomach. "I think I'm gonna..."

She staggered for the bathroom, leaving Nate to head downstairs. So far, so good.

Carmen didn't look as if she'd gotten much rest either. Her shoulders slumped forwards, and she yawned as Nate opened the shop door.

"Sleep well?" he asked.

"Like a baby." Why did people always say that? Didn't babies wake up crying every half hour? "How about you? Your Casanova act worked on Verónica?"

"I doubt she'll be leaving the bedroom today."

"Don't you feel guilty for playing with her emotions like that?"

For buying her expensive drinks, then letting her think she'd got what she wanted? Not really.

"It's part of the job. Are you sure you're ready for this?"

"Just give me the damn costume."

Nate desperately wanted to dig deeper, to find out who she'd been talking about last night, but he didn't dare, not when she needed all her faculties to deal with her visit to Lozano. So he shut up and went to Verónica's workroom, where he'd watched her pack Lozano's skeleton-embellished suit, black on white, into a garment cover yesterday. His shoes had gone into a separate bag, the mask into a cardboard box. She'd gathered the whole lot into a wheeled case together with a sewing kit and a fragrance sachet, and Nate made one final check to ensure the gloves were in there. Yes, there they were, clipped to the hanger.

"You need to spray the first component of the poison into the gloves just before you get to Lozano's place," Nate reminded Carmen as he handed her the case and Verónica's car keys.

"We've been through this twenty times. Shouldn't you run back to your love nest now?"

Carmen had dressed for the occasion in a black shift dress and heels, hair fastened back in a sleek chignon. The sugar skull broach was pinned above her left breast, a touch of the macabre on an otherwise unmemorable outfit.

He ignored her comment and tapped his ear. "Remember I'm listening."

"How could I forget?"

With Carmen on her way, all Nate could do was wait. Upstairs, Verónica stumbled out of the bathroom, wiping her mouth, as he returned to his spot on the couch.

"Feeling better?" he asked.

"No. Who was at the door?"

"Some guy in a black Mercedes. Said Mr. Lozano wanted to leave for the parade earlier than planned, so he stopped by to pick up the costume and save you the trouble of delivering it."

"You gave it to him?"

"The one in the bag? Yeah. He checked it was the right one before he took it."

"And he was happy?"

"Seemed that way."

"Thank goodness. I don't need to get up now."

Nate held out the pills he'd brought up earlier. "How about you take a couple of these and go back to sleep? I'll wake you if anybody else comes."

"There shouldn't be anyone. I only open on Saturdays by appointment."

He snaked an arm around her waist and pulled her close. She kissed him with all the passion of a dead fish, then closed her bloodshot eyes.

"Perhaps bed is a good idea."

The best she'd had so far. "Here, let me help you."

Nate listened in Verónica's kitchen, hairs prickling on the back of his neck as Carmen purred up Lozano's driveway in Verónica's Honda. Five minutes until their part would be over, and Lozano's fate would be in the hands of, well, fate.

The engine fell silent. A door slammed. *Crunch, crunch, crunch.* That must have been Carmen walking over the gravel.

Finally, a doorbell rang, a great clanging thing that shouted its owner's self-importance.

"Can I help?"

"I'm here to deliver Señor Lozano's costume for the parade."

"We're expecting Señorita Camacho. Where is she?"

"Sick. Really sick. But she didn't want any delays with the costume, so she asked me to bring it. I'm her assistant."

"Your name?"

"Josefina Cortes."

"One minute."

The door closed again, and Verónica's phone rang ten seconds later. Fortunately, Nate had anticipated this, and his old friend at the CIA was already waiting on the other line. All he had to do was answer and hold the two phones together.

"Hello?"

"Señorita Camacho?"

"*Si*," Yolanda said, coughing for effect. "Who is this?"

"I'm an associate of Miguel Lozano's."

"Is there a problem with the costume?"

"We were expecting you to bring it."

"I've been ill all night, and I know how much Señor Lozano hates germs, so I sent my assistant. I assure you, Josefina's very capable. But if it's a problem, just send her back and I'll come myself."

The guy paused. Lozano hated people deviating from his plans, but who would want to be responsible for making the boss sick? Luckily not this goon.

"No, it's fine. She can do the final fitting."

He hung up, and a cold dread settled in Nate's stomach. Final fitting? What final fitting? Nobody had mentioned that.

"Come in, Señorita Cortes. Señor Lozano will see you now."

No, no, no! For fuck's sake, Carmen, don't go. Just make an excuse and leave.

But of course she didn't. Because Nate's woman was crazy—a barrel short of a gun.

"Thank you. It'll be a pleasure to meet him."

CHAPTER 14 - CARMEN

SHIT, SHIT, SHIT. This was *not* part of the plan.

After a cursory pat-down, I followed Lozano's henchman deeper and deeper into the house. Being a drug lord certainly paid well—everywhere I looked, I saw original paintings and expensive furniture. And people. Eight guards, three maids, even a freaking butler. Would I like a drink? No thanks, I just wanted to get out of there as fast as possible.

And then we reached Lozano's dressing room. The man himself stood centre stage in his underwear, and he didn't bother to disguise his leering gaze as he looked me up and down.

"Ah, a younger model. You work for Verónica?"

"That's right."

He pointed at a chair. "Sit."

I was so, so tempted to call him out on his lack of manners, but I couldn't afford to. Not alone in his house, with a tiny brooch my only connection to the outside world. I hadn't even brought a gun in case they searched me. So I sat.

Lozano was forty-seven years old, more than double my age, and he'd gone soft around the middle, but from the way he preened in front of me, I guessed I wasn't supposed to care about that. He put on the white shirt, then the suit with its bone detail embroidered in black.

I might've admired the tailoring if I wasn't trying so hard to keep my breathing under control.

"The pants are too tight. You will have to move the button."

Good thing *mi abuela* had taught me to sew when I was a little girl. I knew there was a sewing kit in the case, because I'd seen it earlier when I sprayed the gloves.

"Okay, I can do that."

I expected him to take the pants off, but no, he just stood there, grinning while I got to my knees in front of him. Tell me he didn't expect extras.

"Perhaps you see something you like down there?"

"Please keep still. I don't want to sew the button to your testicles by accident."

A lie—I'd have enjoyed doing exactly that.

Lozano roared with laughter. "Ah, a feisty girl. This is good."

"Just being honest."

I cut the button away as fast as I could and began stitching it back on half an inch further out.

"So few people are honest with me now. Mostly, they tell me what they think I want to hear."

"That's because they're afraid of you shooting them, or so I've heard."

Another guffaw. "See? You're refreshing. What are you doing this afternoon?"

"This afternoon? I'm going to the parade."

"*Perfecto*. You can come with me."

And sit in a room filled with sarin gas? No thanks.

"I'm going with my fiancé."

"You're engaged?"

"That's generally what having a fiancé means. Señor

Lozano, I asked you not to move. Unless you like body piercings?"

"That mouth will get you into trouble one day. Has anybody ever told you that?"

"More times than I can count." I knotted the end of the thread. It wasn't the world's best sewing job, but my customer would be dead soon, so I figured that didn't matter so much. "There. Finished."

"Are you sure I can't persuade you to rethink my invitation?"

"Positive. But enjoy the parade. Every year, it brings new surprises."

"Indeed it does. If you change your mind, I'm sure you can get my number from Señorita Camacho."

"I'm afraid that won't happen."

Lozano beckoned to one of the guards hovering in the doorway. Even in the house, security was tight.

"Please see Señorita Cortes out."

Nobody spoke as we trailed back through the house, and I half expected to be stopped at any moment, to be hauled back in to face Lozano when he realised what I'd done. I still couldn't believe what had just happened. Perhaps I should have been more deferential, but when he practically shoved his crotch in my face, I just couldn't bring myself to be polite.

One guard followed me all the way to the car while three more watched from the doorway. They'd searched the vehicle; I could tell from a glance. I'd deliberately left a peso lined up straight in the coin tray in the centre console, and now it had been moved. But never mind—there was nothing for them to find. The gates opened silently when I reached the end of the driveway, and I turned right at a leisurely pace.

My first attempt at a close-up assassination, and I'd survived.

I was free.

Well, sort of. Three miles along the road, I glanced in the rear-view mirror and Nate glared back at me from his SUV. Why was he so angry? What had I done?

A quarter mile passed, and he still looked furious. I wanted to keep driving, but I put on the turn signal and pulled off the road. Five seconds later, he climbed into the passenger seat, then bristled as he leaned across the centre console.

"What the hell were you playing at?"

"Assassinating a drug lord?"

"You know exactly what I mean. You weren't supposed to go inside."

"When they invited me, I could hardly decline, could I? Verónica wouldn't have."

"Anything could have happened in there."

"But it didn't, so stop yelling at me. I did my job, okay? I handled it. He asked me to suck his damn cock, and I declined."

"You could have antagonised him with that smart fucking mouth of yours."

"Some men like my smart mouth."

"I know."

I glared at him. Kept glaring until he backed off a few inches. Finally, he broke eye contact.

"I'm sorry. When you went inside, I got nervous. I didn't know whether to stay back and freak out or try to get in and rescue you."

"How about neither? I can look after myself."

"I know that too. It's just... I was worried, and I'm not used to that."

Neither was I. Not used to worrying about someone, or being worried about. But Nate stirred up all these unfamiliar feelings I wasn't sure what to do with other than to pretend they didn't exist. He'd be gone in two days max. If I let myself care, I'd only get hurt.

"Why don't we go to the parade?" I suggested. Right now, we both needed a distraction. "You've got a costume from Verónica, and I can pick one up at the store."

His rigid posture softened a little. "I never normally like to hang around the scene of the crime, but I guess this time we won't stick out, not with thousands of other people there."

"Have you ever been to the parade before?"

"It's not normally my kind of thing."

"Then let's take this car back and pop your Día de los Muertos cherry. You never know—you might even enjoy it."

Chapter 15 - Carmen

I SHOPPED FOR a costume while Nate stayed at Verónica's for another hour in case of any last-minute Lozano-related hiccups. Or so he said. I still had a niggling fear that he liked her, and every time I imagined the two of them together last night, I couldn't decide whether to choke on the lump in my throat or hit something.

He drives a Porsche, I reminded myself. *He's not your type anyway.*

But he'd still come for me when he thought I might be in trouble.

I pushed him out of my head as I selected a short black dress with a layer of dark-pink chiffon over the skirt and roses around the edge of the corset top. A white half-mask completed the ensemble, trimmed with more roses and painted with colourful dots and swirls. Nate's outfit would be far more ornate, seeing as Verónica had created it, but I'd given up caring. My job was done. All I wanted to do was crawl home and drown my sorrows in tequila. Wherever home was. The army base felt more distant with every passing day, and I didn't want to go back and live with my parents either. After five years away, it would be the ultimate failure. No, I'd have to find a place of my own. I had savings, but if I wasn't working, that—

My phone rang. Nate.

"I'm done here. Can you pick me up?"

Seeing as he had to go back to Verónica's, we'd swapped cars after our little tête-à-tête, and I had his rented SUV. And his wallet with a pile of cash. He'd told me to spend whatever I wanted. At first, I found it odd the way he trusted me, but then I figured that since we'd plotted a murder together, me stealing a few pesos probably wasn't something he worried about.

"I'm on my way."

"Did you get something to wear?"

"There wasn't much left, but yes."

The first thing Nate said when he climbed into the car was, "Let's go back to the apartment."

"What? Why?"

"Because you're wearing thigh-high stockings and a dress that barely covers your ass."

"I told you they didn't have much left."

And I liked the stockings. They had leg bones printed on them, and all the people who'd watched me try them on said they looked good.

"We're supposed to be keeping a low profile. If you go out like that, every man in a three-block radius will be watching you."

"I won't be the only person dressed this way. And I always go to the parade. If you don't want to go with me, I can drop you off first."

"If you're going, I'm going."

"Then stop complaining. And smile."

The instant we got out of the car, Nate grasped my hand, and I couldn't say I minded. He made me feel safe, protected, and even though I was capable of looking after myself, it was nice to share the load. The parade was in full swing, and we had to fight our way through the crowds as the floats went past, followed by dancers and bands and acrobats.

"Why don't we watch from here for a while?" I asked. My shoes had also been a last-minute purchase, and I'd gone for style rather than comfort.

"Sure."

I stiffened as Nate moved behind me and wrapped his arms around my waist.

"What are you doing?"

"Stopping the rest of the male population from staring at your ass."

Maybe so, but that didn't stop all the women from staring at his. His suit was the reverse of Lozano's, black with white embroidery and a blood-red shirt, and I almost offered to adjust the button on the pants for him. I wouldn't have minded a faceful of Nate. But he seemed more interested in the people around us than me, so I had to take what I could get while we waited for Lozano to eat lunch.

That was the genius of Nate's plan. We didn't need to add the second part of the binary agent because Lozano would do it himself. The mixture on the inside of the gloves would be activated by isopropyl alcohol, you see, and Lozano covered himself in the stuff before every meal when he used his hand sanitiser. Once the two ingredients reacted, they'd create enough sarin gas to kill him.

First his nose would run, then his eyes would water, and he'd start to drool and vomit as acetylcholine built up in his body and prevented his neurotransmitters from working properly. His vision would blur. He'd piss himself and shit himself, and since sarin has no taste or smell, he wouldn't even know why. A few minutes later, he'd convulse and die, and by the time doctors reached him, delayed by the crowds and the traffic around the parade, the gas would have evaporated.

A nasty way to die, but since he'd been responsible for so many murders in Mexico over the past few years, I couldn't bring myself to care.

But you'd better believe I scrubbed my hands after I sprayed that stuff inside Lozano's gloves.

"What time is it?" I asked Nate.

He held up his wrist, and I tilted it so I could make out the hands on his watch under the sun's glare. Twelve fifty-seven. Three minutes to go if Lozano stuck to the timetable.

I fidgeted in Nate's arms, and he hugged me tighter, brushing a thumb over my hip bone.

"Shh. If it happens, it happens. Otherwise we'll try again."

"I might not have a job if it doesn't happen."

"You'll have a job. I'll give you a job."

"What do you mean, you'll— Oh shit."

Out of the corner of my eye, I saw my ex walking towards us. Antonio *el acosador* as Teo had named him. The stalker. He may not have seen me yet, but he would. The creep had some sort of weird radar that homed in on me whenever he was nearby.

"What's wrong?" Nate asked.

"My ex-boyfriend is walking towards us. Fuck."

Far from tensing up like me, Nate seemed to relax. "Is he the guy you hate?"

"Huh?"

"Last night, you said you hated somebody. Was that

him?"

I racked my brains, and a chill ran through me when I remembered. Those three words. *I hate you.* And if Nate had heard me say them, he must also have heard what came before. My gasps. My groans of pleasure as I got myself off thinking about him. His cock, specifically. Dreaming of how it would fit so perfectly between my legs.

"How did you...?"

My cheeks heated, and I wished I'd worn make-up as well as a mask. The most embarrassing moment of my life, and I wanted to run to the end of the earth but my feet wouldn't move.

Nate cupped one hand over the sugar skull broach, which I'd pinned to my left breast again.

"It was transmitting."

"Just kill me now."

"Carmen, who do you hate? This clown?"

"No, you. I hate you, okay?"

Now his grip loosened. "I thought we'd gotten past that."

"Well, we haven't. I hate the way you make me feel. All strange and needy. I hate that I can't stop thinking about you. And I hate that I felt so jealous when you slept with Verónica."

"I didn't sleep with Verónica."

"You didn't?"

"I drugged Verónica and spent the whole night on her sofa thinking of you."

Okay, so I shouldn't have condoned drugging another woman, but when Nate said that, my heart kind of swelled and hammered against my ribcage.

"Carmen? Is that you?" Antonio asked.

See? I told you he'd spot me, even with the half-mask on. And desperation kicked in. I twisted in Nate's arms and did the only thing I could think of—a burst of insanity that made perfect sense at the time. I pushed his mask up and kissed him.

In my peripheral vision, I saw Antonio stop in his tracks. Then Nate kissed me back and nothing else mattered anymore. Not Antonio, not the parade, not panicked shouts from the VIP area, and not the sirens that wailed in the distance.

"Take me back to the apartment," I whispered.

Nate didn't reply, just picked me up and walked towards the car.

Only *he* mattered.

CHAPTER 16 - NATE

THIS IS GOING to be messy as fuck, in every way possible.

But Nate didn't care, just pushed his way through the crowds as Carmen clung to him. His dirty little sniper, the mouthy firecracker who'd driven him wild since the moment she showed up at his apartment.

Trouble with a capital T, but who cared when she tasted as sweet as she did? The men at GAFE were all wrong about her. She could do more than shoot, and she definitely wasn't frigid. Fuck, she had his pants undone and his cock in her mouth before they got out of the parking lot. Lucky the cops were busy dealing with the aftermath of Lozano or there could have been a problem. As it was, Nate stuck religiously to the speed limit while his feet twitched against the pedals.

He'd gone for an automatic rather than a stick, and now he twisted one hand in Carmen's hair as she sucked. Damn, she was hot. The head of his cock hit the back of her throat as she fondled the base, and he almost missed a red traffic light.

Too late, he realised the driver in the semi truck next to them could see everything. At least, everything but Carmen's face, so that was okay. He just gave the guy a grin and a wave and sped off the moment the light turned green.

"Can't hold on much longer, *querida*."

"Then don't."

He shot his load as they reached the apartment block, and she swallowed like a pro. Who needed to play the lotto? He'd hit the fucking jackpot.

Carmen looked up, dazed. "Are we back?"

"We're back, and you're wearing far too many clothes."

"You said I wasn't wearing enough clothes earlier. Make up your mind."

"Maybe I'll just fuck you in this dress." Nate tucked himself away, strode around to the passenger side and reached underneath the skirt, then tore her panties off and stuffed them into his pocket. "I like the stockings."

At least, he did now they were for his eyes only.

He put one knee to the door sill and leaned in closer, kissing her stupid as he slipped his hand between her legs. Fuck, she was soaked, and he couldn't resist sliding one finger inside.

"Deeper." She gasped and parted for him.

"How about I make you come right here, *querida*? With people walking past outside. Some of them might stop to watch."

"Do it."

Black called Emmy a mental bitch, but Nate had a feeling Carmen would give her a run for her money. Carmen wasn't only crazy, she was filthy—the best possible combination.

And he had his orders. One long kiss later, where she surprised him by biting his damn lip, he added a second finger and she detonated around him.

"Shh." He clamped a hand over her mouth because no matter what he'd said, he really didn't want people watching.

"I don't hate you quite so much anymore."

"Good. Let's go upstairs and work on that, shall we? Because I'm going to fucking ruin you."

She tugged her skirt down as she climbed out of the car, but he still got an eyeful. Glistening pink lips, begging for attention. She wasn't walking fast enough on those ridiculous shoes, so he picked her up again and climbed the stairs, ready to break the door off its hinges when the key wouldn't fit in the lock.

She snatched it from him. "Give it here; I'll do it. You need to learn some restraint."

"I've got restraint. I didn't bend you over the hood in the parking lot."

Carmen slammed the door shut behind them and leaned over the table. "Screw me over this instead."

"It's not strong enough." He threw her onto the bed and fished a condom out of his wallet. "I'm not holding back. Not tonight."

"You'd better not." She stood again and tugged at the strings on the back of her dress, smiling as it loosened and fell to the floor. "Come on, I want a look at the whole package."

Nate raised an eyebrow. "Don't you mean *another* look?"

"Huh?"

"You were watching my reflection the other day."

"Uh..." Fuck, that blush was sexy.

"Why do you think I took so long getting dressed?"

He stripped, pausing to take in all that was Carmen as she stretched out on his bed. Her smooth, tanned skin, her flat stomach, that little triangle of curls leading to the good parts. And when he finally sank his dick into her, he knew that was the only place he ever wanted it to be. He'd finally found his soulmate.

The only question was, how the fuck did they make this relationship work?

CHAPTER 17 - CARMEN

"WHAT TIME IS it?" I asked.

We'd been up all night, fucking and touching and licking and sucking and making love, and I'd lost track of time and space and reality.

Nate turned his watch towards me. "Eleven o'clock."

"And what day is it?"

"Sunday."

Sunday... Sunday... "There's something we need to do today."

"I need to do you. Plus a run to the pharmacy for more condoms. And breakfast. We could both use food."

I sat straight up in bed. "Food! Shit! We're due at my parents' for lunch."

Nate's turn to swear. "Can't we skip it?"

"It's my grandma's last goodbye, or so she thinks."

"*Querida*, those psychics just make stuff up."

"I know that, but if we don't go, Grandma'll be really offended." Plus, she'd promised to make churros for dessert. "It's only a few hours, and then I'm yours for...well, however long you're here."

"Yeah, about that..."

"Lunch starts at twelve. Please?"

He rolled me on top of him and kissed me on the

forehead. Sweet. When he did that, I couldn't hate him at all anymore.

"For you. I'll go for you."

"And Dali. Don't forget my brother still has her. He'll want Pasqual's ring back too."

"Dali. How could I possibly forget the dog? More to the point, what the hell are we going to do with her?"

"I don't know. Do you have a garden back home?"

"Yeah, I've got twenty acres."

"Perfect. Since I'm about to be homeless, she's yours."

"Why are you about to be homeless?"

"I've been considering my future. There's got to be more to life than a job I hate, and I'm not planning to renew my contract at GAFE." I hesitated, unsure whether Nate had been joking the other night when he mentioned a job. "About what you said..."

His phone rang, and I fell silent as he picked it up. What if I was reading more into this than he was? Sure, we had good sex—great sex—but he had a life in America and I could hardly just insert myself into it. What if he hadn't been serious when he mentioned the job, and I pushed him, and he offered me something out of sympathy? That would be a sure way to build up resentment, and... Hold on, what did he just say?

Nate shifted the phone against his ear. "Declared dead at two o'clock? Excellent. Make sure you chill the champagne."

"Lozano died?" I whispered, and Nate nodded. With all that had happened afterwards, I'd barely given our favourite drug lord another thought.

"I'll pack tomorrow," he told the person on the other end of the line. "The courier can take my gun again, and I'll fly back commercial. Emmy did what? Actually, forget it. I don't want to know."

When he hung up, a chill ran through me. Tomorrow. He'd be leaving tomorrow. We only had one day left, and he'd still offered to spend it with my family. The selfish part of me wanted to keep him for myself, but I couldn't let them down.

"Grandma usually has a siesta in the afternoon. We can leave then."

Nate kissed me again, and I nearly said to hell with the celebration. But then he pulled back and smiled.

"Agreed. And tonight, *querida*, you're all mine."

"What now?" I asked my brother, not bothering to hold back my groan.

Teo had rushed out of the house towards us, and now he shoved us behind the tree again. Why did we even bother walking up the path?

"Before you go in there, I just want you to know that this is *not* my fault. I've been busy with rehearsals for the last four days, and nobody told me a thing about it."

Teo was an actor, and his new play opened in three weeks. He'd spent so much time practising his lines, he sounded croaky.

"What isn't your fault?"

"Even Pasqual knew, and if he'd told me, I'd have tried to stop them. Honestly I would've." Teo huffed a little. "I can't believe he didn't tell me."

"Stop them doing what, Teo?"

The front door burst open and the rest of my family

spilled out.

"There she is!" Mamá screeched.

Grandma clutched at her chest, and I thought she was having palpitations again, but then she sighed. "Carmen's going to make a beautiful bride."

"Sorry, what?"

"I tried to tell you," Teo whispered. "Remember Grandma wanted to see at least one of us married before she died? Well, ta-da! You're it."

"I don't understand."

"They've arranged your whole wedding. You get married in the church on the corner at two o'clock, and then we're having a party afterwards."

"Tell me you're joking." My voice rose in pitch, and I pinched myself. A red welt appeared on my arm, but I didn't wake up. "We only got engaged on Tuesday, and that wasn't even real."

"Well, you can't tell Grandma that now. Think of how upset she'd be. She used her savings to buy you both rings."

Nate was laughing. He was fucking laughing, and I turned to him, hands on hips.

"Okay, genius. What do you suggest?"

"Smile as you walk down the aisle, and don't trip over your dress."

"Be serious, you asshole."

His grin faded. "I am."

"We only met a week ago!"

It was Teo's turn to look incredulous. "What?"

"Exactly!"

Meanwhile, Mamá and Grandma advanced towards us across the scrubby grass my father was so obsessed with watering when everyone else put gravel on their yards.

"Did Teo tell you about our surprise?" Grandma asked, looking beside herself with glee.

"He said you arranged a wedding?"

"Isn't it exciting? My granddaughter, getting married."

"But it's too soon."

"Nonsense. Anyone can see how much he loves you."

Nate just stood there, being absolutely no help at all, except his shit-eating grin came back. Fuck my life. I loved my family, truly I did, but why did they have to interfere so much? Only *mi abuela* could think it was a good idea to organise a whole freaking wedding without telling the happy couple anything about it.

I grabbed hold of Nate's arm.

"Excuse us. I just need to have a word with Nate in private."

"Don't be too long," Mamá said. "You know Father Aguilar hates to be kept waiting."

With the house undoubtedly full of wedding preparations, I shoved Nate back into the car and slammed the door.

"You're not fucking helping."

"What do you want me to do?"

"I don't know—start the engine and keep driving until we get to, say, Brazil?"

"Costa Rica's nicer at this time of year."

"Great. Let's go."

"Sure. Tomorrow morning."

"You can't truly be thinking of going through with this?"

"Why not? I'm gonna marry you someday. Might as

well do it now and make your grandma happy."

"Back up. Back up! What are you talking about?"

Nate gave a lopsided shrug. "Remember the other day when you told me you sold a diamond bracelet to buy a gun?"

"Sort of. Yeah, I guess."

"Well, that was the moment I realised I'd fallen in love with you, and my feelings aren't going to change."

"You what?"

"I fell in love with you."

Holy hell, this was deep.

Nate loved me.

If I said "I do," everything would change in the space of an afternoon. My world had already been tilted on its axis this week, but although Nate had blasted his way into my life like a fucking stormtrooper, he'd also challenged me. While I'd gotten angry when he'd tried to hold me back, knowing what I knew now, I could see he'd only done it because he cared. Plus, I'd learned from him. He hadn't questioned my abilities the way my colleagues did.

And then there was the sex...

I pressed my legs together and forced myself to focus, because I absolutely shouldn't be making this decision with my vagina. Could I really get married to a man I'd known for less than a month?

"You said something about a job for me before. What did you mean?"

"I part-own a security company, Blackwood, and it's growing. We've got one woman at the top, and we could use another. I'd like to train you to work with me."

"What would I have to do?"

"That's up for negotiation, but ideally, some sniping

plus the occasional contract like the one we just worked on."

"You'd want me to continue as an assassin?"

"Yes."

"Would I be able to turn down jobs if I didn't agree with them?"

"Absolutely."

That was more freedom than I had at the moment, plus I'd get Nate.

"Where would I live? With you?"

"That's what husbands and wives tend to do."

Husband and wife. *Joder.* I was twenty-three years old, and my longest relationship had lasted two months. "We barely know each other. I mean, don't you have family you'd want to invite to a wedding?"

"No."

"None?"

"My family doesn't give a shit about me, and the feeling's mutual. I've got a few close friends, but they'll understand if we go ahead and get married today."

"What if we don't? What then?"

"Up to you. Either you could come with me anyway, or we could try something long-distance. I'd visit as often as I could, but I've put too much into Blackwood to just walk away. Fuck." He scrubbed a hand through his hair, the first sign I'd seen that this was as difficult for him as it was for me. "When I came here a month ago, I had no idea this would happen."

Instead of panicking about the upheaval that would follow if I married Nate, I thought of my future if I turned him down. I wouldn't get a better job than the one he'd offered me, so I'd take it—I knew that much. And if I was in America, I'd want to be in his bed every night, even if I didn't get much sleep. We'd argue—that much was obvious from the time we'd spent together so far—but I'd never be the compliant little woman at home, and I didn't want that kind of man either. No, we'd argue, and then we'd compromise.

If Nate drove a Porsche, he wasn't poor, and I wasn't rich, so he wouldn't be after my savings. Not like the guy who took me out to the most expensive restaurant in town a year ago, then stiffed me with the bill.

With Nate, I felt more like an equal. And shacking up with him in Virginia without a ring on my finger would have one big downside—the extra difficulty in getting a visa. It wasn't as if I could list *occupation: assassin* on my application, was it? Marriage would no doubt ease that process.

Meanwhile, Nate was sitting quietly, watching me, giving me space to think.

I liked that.

"Let's do it."

He raised an eyebrow. "Are you sure?"

"You're not having second thoughts?"

"About you, *querida*? Never." He took my hand and kissed my knuckles softly. "Ready to become Mrs. Wood?"

"Are you ready to become Señor Hernandez?"

He broke into a smile and chuckled. "Father Aguilar doesn't like waiting."

"You're such an asshole, *huevitos*."

He dropped my hand into his lap. "You may want to rethink that nickname."

I gave him a squeeze. "Fine. *Huevos grandes.* Happy?"

"Yeah. Yeah, I think I am."

"I now pronounce you husband and wife. You may kiss the bride."

Nate did, and we didn't hold back on the tongues.

"Get a room," Teo yelled.

I gave him the finger, and my grandma gasped in shock. "Carmen! Be nice to your brother."

Since he was the one who'd gotten me into this situation in the first place, I ignored them both, although the suggestion of a room wasn't a bad one. Nate had delayed his flight back, and at least we still had the apartment until the end of the week, because I'd need that time to sort out the inevitable mayhem at work. Nate knew some people at the Secretariat of National Defense, and he'd promised to help, although he confessed they probably wouldn't be too happy with him either. Apparently, the generals thought more highly of me than Captain Pendejo did, and Nate said they'd be upset to lose me.

I didn't care. They should have treated me better.

Earlier, I'd walked down the aisle in my grandma's wedding dress, pinned and stitched together in strategic places. The zipper didn't entirely do up since I had a bigger bust than her, so a hurriedly bought shawl completed the ensemble. At least the rings both fitted. That was a minor miracle.

Pasqual had kept his promise with the flowers, and they were everywhere. Mamá kept sneezing, and Grandma wore a stargazer lily tucked behind one ear. Even Nate had a carnation tucked in his buttonhole—

luckily, he still had a suit stashed at the apartment that we'd rushed back to pick up.

Mrs. Wood. I tried the name out for size, and it felt strange but right at the same time. Carmen Wood.

My husband, Nate Wood.

Fuck.

And now he wrapped an arm around my waist, his hand lingering at the top of my ass in the way that had become oh-so-familiar. I leaned into him, feeling our strength combine into a sum greater than either of us alone. Synergy.

"How much longer do you want to stay?" I asked.

"As long as you want. You've got a good family. And I understand from your grandma that one of the neighbours has baked a cake."

"Yes, Guadalupe Pineda. She's in her nineties, and trust me when I say you don't want to eat it. We'll probably have to cut it with a machete."

"I've got one in the car."

"Why doesn't that surprise me?"

Dali bounded up to us, wearing a bandana and a mini sombrero, followed by Pasqual. The little dog had filled out in the last week, and the tail she'd once kept tucked between her legs now helicoptered in all directions.

"Dali! Don't jump on Carmen's dress," he scolded her. "Come and eat your treats."

"Pasqual adores that puppy, you know," Teo said, sidling up to us as Pasqual led Dali towards the kitchen. "She's been sitting in the shop with him and riding in the passenger seat of his van when he makes deliveries. He'll be devastated when you take her to America with you. That's where you'll live, isn't it?"

Nate and I looked at each other, and we both nodded at the same time.

"I'm moving to Virginia," I told Teo. "But if Pasqual wants to keep Dali, he can. We rescued her from a bad situation last Sunday, so he's spent more time with her than we have."

"Really? We can keep her?"

Nate nodded his agreement. "We know you'll both give her a good home."

As Teo ran off to give Pasqual the good news, I mused over how quickly we'd started using "we" rather than "I." And how natural it felt. Yes, I'd made the right decision today.

The only grey cloud was seeing Grandma's happiness fade towards the end of the evening. She'd smiled all through the service and dinner, but when the younger guests got up to dance, an air of melancholy settled over her.

"How are you feeling?" I asked, squashing down the lingering annoyance at the mayhem she'd caused. "Tired?"

"Just sad that my life will soon be coming to an end."

I clutched her hands in mine. "Thank you for helping me to start my life afresh, *abuela*. And for organising the party today."

"I'm glad to see you happy, little one. And that man of yours is a real hunk. If only I were fifty years younger..."

Well, we all knew where I got my dirty mind from, didn't we?

"When I'm fifty years older, I want to be just like you."

CHAPTER 18 - CARMEN

"GOOD WORK ON Lozano. I'm assuming that was you and not natural causes?"

High praise indeed from Captain Pendejo. "Yes, it was me."

"How did you do it?"

"Poison."

"What kind of poison?"

"I'll keep that to myself."

"Cabo Hernandez, I'm your commanding officer."

Not for long. "I understand that, sir, but as our general once said, it's better to maintain plausible deniability."

He stared at me for a long beat. "Yes, I suppose you're right." His tone said he really hated that idea. "But you'll be pleased to hear that I've decided to give you more responsibilities. This Friday, you'll be travelling to Sonora with five other members of the team. Santino Galegos was spotted there last week, and we understand he'll be trying to muscle in now Lozano's out of the picture."

"How long will I be in Sonora for?"

"A month. Maybe two."

"But my contract ends in three weeks."

"You'll be renewing, yes?"

"No."

He turned into a statue, skin mottled like marble and his coffee cup paused halfway to his mouth. "No? What do you mean, no?"

"I got married at the weekend, and I'm moving to the United States."

"*You?* Married to an *American*?"

Why did he sound so damn surprised? Was it because I'd somehow betrayed my country by hooking up with a foreigner, or the mere thought that I might not be the glacial virgin he'd always assumed?

I shrugged, a gesture reminiscent of my dear husband. "Yes."

Captain P shook his head, as if this scene were a figment of his imagination. "Where am I meant to find another sniper in three weeks?"

"I'm sure being the resourceful man that you are, you won't have any problems."

And perhaps if he'd kept up to date on his paperwork or spoken to me as a person or taken his head out of his own ass occasionally, my departure wouldn't have been such a shock. I had no sympathy whatsoever.

"Are you being sarcastic?" he asked.

"Of course not, sir."

He shuffled some papers around, and his mouth set into a hard line. "Then you leave me no choice but to change my plans. The day after tomorrow, you will go to the south instead."

"The south?"

"Yes, Carmen. The army battalion in Campeche needs help to disrupt drug supply routes." Those thin lips curved into a nasty grin. "Don't forget your bug spray."

"It might not be as bad as you think, *querida*."

Nate glanced up from his laptop as I paced the apartment, stepping around the piles of luggage he'd already packed.

"They don't need me in Campeche. We don't even have a GAFE team there. Captain Pendejo's just doing it to spite me."

"Captain Pendejo?" Nate chuckled. "I like that."

"I'd like it more if he was the one heading south to get eaten alive in the jungle. Last time I was there, I got bitten fifty-seven times. And the mosquito spray melted my shoes. Fuck only knows what it does to my skin."

"If I was a mosquito, I'd pick you too."

My eyes rolled all of their own accord. "You're so damn romantic."

"Three weeks and it'll be over."

"The longest three weeks of my freaking life."

Nate caught my hand as I walked past and smiled as he brought it to his lips. "Stay positive." He closed the laptop and pulled me closer so I nestled between his legs. "Want me to take your mind off things?"

I nodded. It wasn't only my upcoming trip, but also the call I'd just received from Grandma. One last goodbye because she thought she wouldn't wake up tomorrow. I tried to stay upbeat, but it was hard to offer comfort when she sounded so miserable.

The noise of my zipper broke me out of my thoughts, and Nate pushed his computer to the side before lifting me onto the table. I'd have married him for that magic tongue alone. Ten minutes later, I'd forgotten Captain P and drug smugglers and family and my move to the US. I only cared about that little knot of nerves between my legs and what my husband was doing to it. Fuck. My back arched off the table as stars burst behind my eyes, and before I came back down to earth, Nate carried me over to the bed. Staying in a tiny apartment had definite advantages.

We'd barely spoken about my new home in Virginia, only that it was being renovated and the heating didn't totally work right now. Nate had promised to keep me warm at night, so I figured I could live with that. And at least I wouldn't need to share a bathroom with nineteen men, most of whom had problems judging distance. In the end, I'd taped up a laminated sign: *Please stand closer to the toilet—your* pija *isn't as long as you think.*

Fortunately, Nate didn't appear to suffer from either of those problems.

And now he rolled me over to straddle him, and I had to smile at the view. Only three more weeks until I could wake up to that every morning.

The olive-green plane stood on the tarmac, a drab homage to functionality over style in the shimmering heat haze. Everything I needed for my time in Campeche fitted in my backpack, including the extra-large bottle of bug repellent and the mosquito net Nate had given me as parting gifts. And the cookies from Grandma. Yes, she'd woken up fit and healthy on Tuesday morning, if a little sheepish after her dramatic declarations of the previous six months. I hadn't entirely forgiven her for the wedding surprise, but I was getting there, especially after spending two more nights with Nate.

I hefted my rifle case as I climbed the steps, hoping I wouldn't have to use the army-issued HK PSG1 in anger on this operation. A nice, easy trip—that was what I wanted. No paperwork. My beloved AWM was in Nate's care, waiting to be shipped back to the US with his CheyTac and the crate of other belongings I wanted to take with me. He'd be leaving too, for a short job in Washington State, but he'd promised to come back to Mexico so we could fly to Virginia together. Funny how quickly I'd gotten used to the idea of him being around. Other than Teo, nobody had ever waited for me to step off the plane, and my heart skipped just thinking about it. For the first time, a few butterflies fluttered in my stomach—what if his friends back home didn't like me?

Don't start, Carmen. Focus on the job.

I ran through my mental checklist as I slumped into the uncomfortable canvas seat. Gun: check. Ammo: check. Clean underwear: check. Sunglasses: check. Eighteen days to go. Four hundred and thirty-two hours. What was that in minutes? I didn't want to think about it—too long, and I was useless at math unless it involved sniping calculations.

"You're definitely leaving?" Nestor asked. "I thought you'd be in GAFE for life."

"Things change."

"I always felt safer with you at my back."

Really? He'd never said that before. "Thanks, I guess. You're going to Campeche? I thought you were still on medical leave."

Nestor had gotten a stress fracture in his ankle, and

the doctor insisted he rest for six weeks. That was a month ago.

"I was going crazy stuck at headquarters, and the new doctor signed me off."

"New doctor? Is he good?"

"She, and I can't really remember. Everything after the first bottle of tequila is a blur, but she was smiling the next morning."

You see what I had to work with? "I thought you'd go with one of the other teams this week."

"They didn't need any more people in Chihuahua, and I got the impression Captain Benitez only wanted a select few in Sonora. There's something odd about that guy."

"I was supposed to—"

Heavy footsteps on the metal stairs outside interrupted me. Who else was coming? I thought we were only waiting for the pilot to do his final checks. What the...? A trio of military police marched in, guns at their sides.

"You two. Off the plane."

Nestor stood first. "We're from GAFE. What's going on?"

"Your whole unit has been suspended pending investigation. Would you follow us, please?"

Please. He might have used the word, but there was nothing polite about his request.

"Why are we being suspended? We haven't done anything wrong."

Lozano had been a sanctioned kill, the same as every other one of my victims. And although Nestor was a prick at times, I couldn't think of any rules he'd broken either. He'd been on crutches for the last month, for Pete's sake.

"Tell us what's going on," I demanded. "And show us some ID before you start issuing orders."

I may have been a woman, but I was still GAFE, and the tallest of the policemen paused at my tone.

"We have a directive from the Secretariat of National Defense." He handed over his ID card. "Your captain has been arrested for corruption, and until we find out who else on his team is in league with him, you're all suspended from active duty."

"Corruption?" Nate had mentioned his suspicions of that, but I never thought for a moment they'd actually arrest Captain P. "Are you serious?"

"You need to get off the plane now."

I turned to Nestor, and he shrugged. "Better do what he says. Look on the positive side—we don't have to battle with the mosquitos now."

On the tarmac, I expected to be taken to headquarters along with Nestor to unravel this new mess, but the smallest of the three policemen pointed me towards a separate jeep.

"Where are we going?"

"Just load your equipment into the back. Not the rifle. That stays here."

"But where are you taking me? Why am I not going with my colleague?"

"I've been instructed to drop you at the front gate."

"Why? By who?"

He ignored me and climbed into the driver's side. I wasn't scared, more curious, mainly because I had a gun on my hip and I'd bet a thousand pesos I was faster on the draw than Mr. Charisma behind the wheel.

"Are you taking me for questioning?" I tried again.

Nothing.

At the gate, we pulled over into a space beside the guard building, and my new friend pointed at the road outside.

"Just give me your weapon, and then they'll let you out."

"You want me to leave the base?"

"That's what my orders are."

"I don't understand. Where am I supposed to go?"

He shrugged. Not his problem.

Well, fine. I had my phone, and I had money in the bank. I could call a cab and go to my parents' house. Mamá's food was better than anything the mess hall served up, anyway. Yes, I'd stay at home until somebody graced me with a proper explanation, because if this was how they acted, then they could make the effort to call, not me. Fuck the army and everyone in it.

Except I didn't get that far. When I got past the guard building, I saw a familiar SUV parked at the side of the road, and my feet started running towards it before I'd properly processed what was happening.

"Nate!" I wrenched the door open. "What the hell are you doing here?"

"Picking you up. Get in or we'll miss our flight."

"What the hell is going on?"

"Seat belt, *querida*."

"Will you answer the damn question?"

"You're free. Your service in the army is done, and we're flying to Virginia."

"Today?"

"Today."

"But my family..."

"I already spoke to them, and they're all very happy for us. Your grandma's coming to visit once we've got a spare room with furniture in it."

"She doesn't even have a passport."

"Teo's helping with that."

"Wait. Wait! We can't just leave like this. There's some sort of investigation. They'll have questions. Captain Benitez..."

"Is in jail. I swapped evidence of his collusion with drug cartels for your early release plus future discounts on Blackwood's services. He's not the only corrupt bastard in GAFE, either. Most of the Sonora team is dirty."

Oh my... "Sonora? I was supposed to be going there."

"Fifty bucks says he planned to recruit you. Probably thought you'd be an easy mark."

"I assure you I wouldn't have been."

"Don't worry; I believe you. Emmy aside, you're the most difficult woman I've ever met." He kissed my knuckles—another habit of his I was getting used to. "But I still love you."

Fuck, this man was everything. "I love you too, *huevos grandes*."

CHAPTER 19 - CARMEN

"DELAYED DUE TO technical fault," I read out.

It looked as if we wouldn't be getting to Virginia quite so soon after all, and I didn't know whether to be happy or sad about that. On the one hand, I wanted to see the place, but on the other, the thought of meeting a bunch of strangers made me nervous.

"Want a coffee?" Nate asked.

"Please. What have you told your friends about me? About us?"

Nate's brows pinched together. "Nothing yet. I was too busy trying to get you home."

"They don't even know I'm coming?"

"Nope." He grinned, eyes twinkling. "And Emmy hates surprises. I can't wait to see the look on her face."

"This isn't funny. Nate, you have to tell them."

"I will. Later."

"No, now. Or... Or..." I glanced up at the departures board. "Or I'm flying to Australia. I always wanted to see Sydney Opera House and learn to scuba-dive." Nate closed his eyes and took a couple of deep breaths. Was I getting to him? Good. "You can't just expect me to fall into line every time you get a stupid idea in your head."

His eyes popped open. "Fuck it. Let's both go to Australia."

"Didn't you hear a word I just said?"

"I owe you a honeymoon, and I want to see Sydney Opera House too. Come on, it'll be fun. A hut on the beach, white sand, blue sea, just the two of us. I can teach you to scuba-dive."

Was it crazy that I was actually considering it? The furthest I'd ever travelled was Guatemala, and that was for work.

"Don't you have a job to do this week?"

"Hmm. Two seconds." He pulled out his phone and dialled. "Ray? I need a favour. Put your surfboard down and get your ass to Seattle... No, it's an easy one, and you owe me. Black's got the details... Thanks, buddy." Nate smirked at me. "Not anymore."

Freaking hell, I'd married Mr. Fix-it.

"Fine. I'll go as long as you tell your friends about me. It's not fair to keep them in the dark, especially if I'm supposed to be working at their company."

This time, I got a sigh. "Okay, we'll call them. Let's find somewhere quiet."

"Somewhere quiet" turned out to be a janitor's closet. Nate stole a pass to let us in and turned two buckets upside down for us to sit on.

The phone rang once, twice on speaker.

"Black."

One word, and I shivered at his tone even though he was thousands of miles away. But Nate didn't seem fazed.

"Is Emmy there?"

A pause. "She is now. Why?"

"I've got good news and bad news."

"Benitez is still loose?"

"No, he's locked up, but there's going to be a small delay in my return stateside."

"How much of a delay?"

Nate looked at me and raised an eyebrow.

"A week," I mouthed.

"Two weeks."

Oh, Nate.

"You're kidding me? What about Seattle?"

"Pale's gonna take care of it."

Black snorted down the phone. "Bet he's thrilled."

"Not really, but he's coming anyway."

"So why the delay?"

"I recruited a sniper. She's good."

"She?"

"Carmen Hernandez, formerly of GAFE."

"Okay. I've heard of her. She *is* good, but that still doesn't explain the delay."

Black had heard of me? Really? That was kind of... flattering.

"I also married her."

A choking sound came through the phone, followed by a female laughing her head off.

"Oh, this is brilliant." She was English. I hadn't expected that. "I've never seen Black speechless before. Is Carmen there?"

"Yes," I said, but it came out croaky. I cleared my throat and tried again. "I'm here."

"Congratulations, honey. Promise me you won't take any of Nate's shit."

"I'm not."

Nate grimaced. "Believe me, she's not."

"So the delay is for what? Your honeymoon?"

"We're going to Australia."

"The kangaroos are cute, but watch out for the snakes, spiders, sharks, and jellyfish. Wow. Black's gone white." She laughed. "Do me a favour and bring me back a packet of Tim Tams. I love those things."

I liked her already. "Tim Tams. Those are like cookies, yes?"

"Yup. Chocolate ones."

"Okay, I'll bring them."

"Black's turned a funny shade of green now, and I need to clear up the coffee he spat. Have a good time."

She hung up, and I looked across at Nate.

"Did that go well or badly?"

"About as I expected. Don't worry—we've got Emmy on our side, and she'll deal with Black. Let's go and buy tickets. And bikinis. You need bikinis. And one of those kaftan things for when other men are around."

"I'll wear a bikini if you wear a pair of Speedos."

"On second thoughts, let's rent somewhere with a private beach and go naked."

"I'm not sure my budget runs to a private beach."

"*Querida*, you just earned a million bucks for your part in the Lozano job, and besides, I'm paying."

"A million...? What?"

"Private work pays well." He wrapped one arm around me and tucked me against his side as we snuck out of the closet. "Do you prefer a window seat or an aisle seat?"

If I'd learned one thing during my years at GAFE, it was that there was a time to fight and a time to yield.

And today? I yielded.

Little bits of my new world were filtering into my brain, and I still needed to find my place. But in the meantime, Nate could take over. I was exhausted. Five years in the army had taken their toll, and what better way to relax than on a deserted stretch of sand with a delicious man by my side?

"A window seat. I prefer a window seat."

Picky the Pony

CHAPTER 1

"PLEASE, PICKY, JUST walk. It's almost dark."

I squeezed my pony's sides with my heels, but he stood firm and snorted. *Okay, deep breaths.* We'd been through this rigmarole at least twenty times in the last hour, and as the sun dropped, my pulse raced faster.

How had things gone so wrong? Ever since I was a little girl living in the East End of London, I'd dreamed of unpolluted skies and wide-open spaces. Now I was stuck in the middle of Dartmoor at twilight on my uncooperative four-legged friend, with a dead phone and no idea which way home was.

Fantastic.

Welcome to your new life, Sarah.

Picky finally deigned to walk past the killer twig, and as we headed along another track that looked exactly the same as all the others, I had plenty of time to reflect on how my dream turned into a nightmare. Kevin Simmons. I'd adored him since the day he walked into my sixth-form English class with a battered rucksack slung over one shoulder and that crooked grin on his face. My infatuation continued until the day he asked me out for dinner—well, a cheeseburger—and turned to love by the time we both finished school. It was only natural for us to move in together.

Kevin had worked as a salesman for a software

company in Aldgate while I tried hairdressing, attempted fashion retail, and finally started up my own business as a virtual assistant. Who knew so many companies wanted someone to field phone calls and reply to emails? Not me, and certainly not Kevin. With hindsight, our problems started when my earnings surpassed his.

Picky shook me out of my thoughts as he leapt sideways. I peered into the gloom beside the path, but there was nothing there except a few gorse bushes and a lone crisp packet.

"You ate crisps yesterday. You like crisps. If you go past it, I promise I'll buy you a whole bag all to yourself."

Horses weren't really supposed to eat crisps, that much I knew, but by then I'd have tried anything. He crept past sideways, blowing out air, and we carried on as the sky grew greyer.

Yes, I'd say my decision to move to Dartmoor was forty percent my fault and sixty percent Kevin's. Because when a girl twists her ankle and returns early from yoga class to find her significant other shagging the downstairs neighbour on the sofa they'd carefully chosen as a couple from John Lewis, there's only one thing to do, isn't there? Yes, that's right. Drink a bottle and a half of white wine, scoff a box of chocolates, and buy a dilapidated cottage in an online property auction.

In my defence, the photos attached to the listing had definitely been taken in good light, most likely several years ago. Maybe even several decades.

When I arrived at my new home with my Wi-Fi dongle, my laptop, and all of my other worldly belongings stuffed into the back of my Toyota Prius, I'd spent the first two days crying.

What had I done?

The electrics didn't work properly, the roof leaked, the toilet smelled really, really bad, and somebody had climbed in through one of the broken windows and painted grossly oversized parts of the male anatomy all over the living room. Four months on, I'd had the entire place rewired, and it didn't rain inside anymore, but a lack of funds meant I was tackling the rest of the renovations myself. I'd put six coats of emulsion on the living room wall, but on a sunny day, you could still see two coconuts and a totem pole glowing through next to the fireplace.

Then Picky happened.

I'd always loved horses, and every Christmas my stocking was filled with assorted My Little Pony accessories. Later in life, my Saturday morning riding lessons had been an endless source of tension with Kevin, who'd complained long and loud about the amount of money I spent on "those bloody nags." But even so, I'd never quite intended on buying my own equine.

That second moment of madness had happened on a rainy Thursday afternoon as I drove back from a trip to Exeter to buy bathroom tiles. A little sign by the side of the road invited me to visit the pony auction at Chagford a few miles down the road, and as I'd finished work early for the day, I signalled left and went to explore. It was about time I got to know the local area, wasn't it?

I'd spent so much time in the cottage, either working or attempting to stick the fabric of the building back together using duct tape and silicone sealant, that

I'd barely met any of my neighbours. Mabel in the village shop kept me up to date on any important news, like the state of Mrs. McGreeky's bunions and Sandra Thompson's failed audition for *The Great British Bake Off*, but apart from that, most of my socialising took place on the internet. I'd become a regular on the DIY forums and even started a blog on fifty meals to make without a fully functioning oven.

Yes, I'll admit it—I was lonely.

When I thought of a pony auction, I'd imagined rows of stables, each with a friendly face looking over the door. Shiny horses, groomed to perfection, with a perma-tanned auctioneer extolling their virtues in his plummy accent.

No.

The reality was a muddy ring with a series of grimy, wide-eyed animals alternately plunging around or standing stock-still in fear. Middle-aged men bid on them for a few pounds a go in between scratching their unmentionables and snarfing down chips from the catering van. I wanted to leave, but at the same time, I couldn't. What if a pony didn't get any bids? I'd heard those awful stories about them getting bought for meat.

And then Picky came out. The last lot of the day, a tatty skewbald with his ribs showing through the remains of his fluffy winter coat.

"Lot number forty-two...er..." The auctioneer glanced at his list. "Picnic. Bit of an interloper here in Dartmoor—a New Forest pony, fourteen hands high. Who'll start the bidding at fifty pounds?"

Crickets.

"Nobody? Lovely nag, this one, six years old and broken to saddle as well. Forty pounds?"

Nobody. Not a single hand.

Poor Picnic stood there looking so dejected, his head hanging almost to his knees. But it was his eyes that got me. He'd never known kindness.

"Thirty pounds?"

A man on the other side of the ring raised his hand, seemingly reluctant, and I glimpsed *his* eyes under his tweed cap. They looked as if they didn't know the meaning of kindness either, and my heart broke. So little for a life.

"Thirty-five pounds!"

Good grief. Did I just shout that?

The hammer came down.

"Sold to the lady on my right. Congratulations, love. He'll be a right cracker."

Now what? I'd never had to transport a pony before, but I was fairly sure it wouldn't fit into the boot of a Toyota Prius. I didn't even have a headcollar.

I was still standing there, dazed, when a young lad handed over a piece of frayed baling twine with Picnic attached to the other end and held out his palm for the cash.

"You look confused, lady."

"I'm just not quite sure how I'm going to get him home."

He jerked his thumb to the side. "Try old Joe. He's got a trailer."

Turned out old Joe was delighted to help. For the bargain price of eighty-five pounds, he delivered Picnic on his piece of string right to my garden gate.

"You keeping him in there, love?"

"I think so. Yes. Yes, I am."

"But there's a big hole in the back fence."

I followed his finger as he pointed. So there was. I hadn't ventured outside much, and the garden was enormous. More like a jungle, really, and the inside of the house depressed me quite enough already.

"He was a bit of an impulse buy."

For another thirty pounds, Joe fished around in my tumbledown shed for some old planks, then nailed them over the gap. He waved cheerily as he drove off with my pile of money.

Fantastic.

"Okay, Picnic, it's just you and me. Please don't eat the door handles, and if you could avoid scratching your bottom on my car, I'd be much obliged."

Never again would I act on impulse.

CHAPTER 2

FAST-FORWARD THREE months, and Picnic was a little on the chubby side. He had his own bucket instead of drinking from the washing-up bowl, and thanks to the support of my new buddies on the Horse and Hound internet forum, I'd begun riding him.

Which led us to our current predicament.

Theoretically, it should have been possible for me to navigate by the stars, which were now beginning to twinkle in the rapidly blackening sky. But I didn't know my Polaris from my elbow, so we'd run out of luck there.

"Do you know the way back, boy?"

I'd once read an article about horses and their sense of direction. According to the author, if you gave a pony its head, it would always find its way home. I dropped Picky's reins and crossed my fingers, only for him to take two steps to a particularly juicy clump of grass and start noshing. So much for that idea.

How cold did it get at night? Sure, it was only early September, but I still needed my duvet, and my little portable heater had been on for the last fortnight.

"Picky, just walk, okay? You won't get carrots if we can't find our way home."

Nobody would even notice I was missing. My parents called from their villa in Spain once a week, my clients weren't expecting me online until Monday, a day and a half away, and my nearest neighbour lived a quarter of a mile down the road. How long did it take to die from hypothermia? Would some party of schoolchildren find my skeleton in ten years' time, the tattered—

I flew through the air as Picky took off, twisting his body so I went sideways and landed in a heap by the track.

What the...?

I must be hallucinating. There was no other explanation for it, because now a bush was walking towards me. No, two. Three. Three bushes, with faces and guns.

"Are you all right, miss?"

Well, at least the foliage around here was polite.

"My ankle hurts. I think I landed on it funny."

The front bush swore softly under his breath. "I'm terribly sorry we scared your horse. We're on a military exercise, and he must have spotted us as you came past."

Military? Too late, I recalled the signs warning of manoeuvres in the area.

"You're soldiers?"

"Close—Royal Marines. Was it the guns that gave it away?"

I smiled in spite of the pain. "Something like that."

"Are you able to walk? I'm Matt, by the way, and these reprobates are Dave and Stewart."

"Sarah."

Matt held out a hand, and I gripped it tightly, digging my nails in from the pain as I got to my feet.

"Sorry. My leg's a little sore."

"Shall I call an ambulance?"

I really didn't want to cause a fuss. "I'm sure I'll be fine with a bag of frozen peas. Uh, I don't suppose you saw where my pony went?"

Dave pointed behind me. "He's over there, eating grass."

Whoever named him Picnic must have known he was ruled by his stomach. "Would one of you be able to help me back on board? And maybe point me in the right direction? We're actually a bit lost."

I gave them my address and Matt's brow crinkled. "You're about four miles away and heading south instead of north."

"Oops."

He passed his gun to Stewart, then began stripping off the outer layers of his camouflage outfit.

"Sergeant, can you radio in to say I'm taking the lady home? She shouldn't be out alone at this time, especially with a dodgy ankle."

I opened my mouth to protest then thought the better of it. Without his help, I'd probably get lost again, and one of their colleagues would trip over my frozen corpse in a few weeks' time.

"No problem. Need a hand, sir?"

"I'll manage. You carry on with the exercise."

I worried that Picky might run away, but he let Matt take his reins and followed like an angel as they walked back over.

"Do you need a leg up?"

"You know horses?"

"Grew up on a farm in Lancashire, and my two sisters rode."

"You didn't?"

"I preferred the tractor."

Matt helped me back into the saddle then fished a GPS unit out of his pocket. "Right, this way."

"Won't you get in trouble with your boss for doing this?"

"On this exercise, I *am* the boss. There's a bunch of Marines out here, and our job is to hunt them down. I've always preferred being in the field to behind a desk, so I join in where I can, but this is the first time I've managed to catch a horse rather than a new recruit."

"I've never fallen off him before. Usually, he doesn't have so much energy."

"Have you owned him for long?"

"Three months, but when I bought him, he wasn't healthy enough to ride."

"Is that a regular thing? Buying sick horses?"

"Not for normal people."

The whole sorry story came tumbling out, mainly because if I kept talking, it took my mind off the pain. By the end, Matt was laughing.

"It's not funny. This is my life. And I keep doing it. Buying things on impulse, I mean. Before Picky, it was the cottage."

"What do you mean?"

"I bought it on the internet after indulging in a tiny bit too much wine. The toilet didn't even flush. What kind of crazy person buys a house without a working toilet?"

Me, that was who. I was a walking disaster, except now I couldn't even walk properly.

"I've driven past that cottage once or twice. Always thought it looked quite nice from the outside. Quaint."

"Right now, I'd prefer somewhere with carpets and central heating."

"It's that bad?"

"I'm doing it up one room at a time. So far, I've got a bedroom and bathroom, and I'm fixing the kitchen as best I can. Things got a bit delayed when Picky arrived."

"Look on the bright side—once you've finished, it'll be all yours and exactly as you want it."

"It's that whole 'finished' part that seems like a pipe dream. How about you? Do you live nearby?"

"I'm based at the Commando Training Centre near Lympstone, so not too far away."

"How long have you been in the Marines?"

"Ten years now. Joined up when I was eighteen."

Which made him three years older than me, and he'd accomplished so much more in his life. Four miles went by faster than I ever thought they would as we chatted, and almost before I realised where we were, Matt pushed open the creaky gate to my garden.

"Does Picky live in here?"

"Yes, at the moment. I need to mend the shed for him before winter so he's got shelter. There's a hole in the side."

But the extra work was worth it. Picky kept me company, and I liked talking to him out of the kitchen window each morning, apart from the time he stuck his head inside and ate my banana.

Matt closed the gate behind us. "Here, I'll help you down."

I slithered off the side, and Matt lowered me gently onto the stone wall that ran along the front of my property. He spoke quietly to Picky, and I felt slightly guilty as he took off the saddle and bridle by himself and stacked them by the cottage's front door.

"Where's your key?"

"In my pocket. Hang on."

I handed it over, and Matt carried me inside. For the first time, I felt embarrassed by my home. Up until then, I'd mostly felt miserable, interspersed with the occasional burst of pride when I got something done, but never embarrassed. Now, the rickety table I'd picked up at a thrift store looked tatty, and the sunshine-yellow tea towels I'd chosen to brighten the place up only served to highlight the rusty hooks they hung on.

And Matt? In the light from the bare bulb, I got a better look at him, and I had to bite my lip to keep from sighing. The man had muscles on top of muscles, and when he bent to put Picky's saddle on a chair, his trousers stretched tight across an ass made for squeezing.

"Need a hand to climb the stairs?"

"No!" Have him see the dirty laundry I'd undoubtedly forgotten to throw in the hamper? No way. "I mean, no thank you."

He smiled, and even under all the brown-and-green paint on his face, I could see his chiselled jaw and high cheekbones. Kind eyes. He had kind eyes too.

"Do you need painkillers?" He crossed to the freezer and began rummaging. "You've got three kinds of ice cream but no peas?"

"The strawberry flavour has real fruit in it."

Kind eyes, but he'd just rolled them.

"This sweet corn should do the trick."

Before I could stop him, he'd crouched in front of

me and pulled off my boot. Please, somebody put me out of my misery. Quite possibly the hottest guy I'd ever met, and my sock had dancing unicorns and a hole in one toe. Please, say my feet didn't smell too bad.

Gentleman that he was, he didn't say a thing or even wrinkle his nose as he took a bandage out of a pouch on his belt and strapped up my ankle, complete with the makeshift ice pack.

"Do you want me to make you something to eat?" he asked.

"I'll be fine, honestly. I've got a stack of microwave meals in the fridge and plenty of ice cream."

"Yeah. Ice cream." His lips flickered into a smile for a second, and then it was gone. "Well, if you're sure you're okay... I should get back to the exercise. Prisoners to take and all that."

"Of course. Thanks for everything."

"See you."

He disappeared, closing the door behind him, and I felt more depressed than ever. I bet Matt had women falling at his feet on a regular basis, only not quite so literally.

Forget it, Sarah.

It wasn't as if I knew his number. I couldn't even call him on the pretence of thanking him for his help again, all *I can never repay you, but please accept this three-course candlelit dinner as a token of my appreciation.*

Yes, I had candles, but soup followed by microwaved spaghetti bolognese and three kinds of ice cream didn't exactly scream romantic, did it?

Romantic? Good grief. How hard *did* I bang my head when I fell off?

CHAPTER 3

WAS THAT A knock at the door or something else in the house breaking? The gutter had fallen off last week and bumped against the wall, and it sounded kind of similar. But today's *clonk* was definitely more of a knock, even though I hadn't had a single visitor since I moved to Devon.

Darn it, I really should check.

A day had passed since my accident, but I still couldn't move very fast on my swollen foot, so it took me a minute to cross the kitchen. By then, a man was peering through the window, and his face looked remarkably familiar.

Was it...? No way. It couldn't be.

I blinked a couple of times, but nothing changed. Matt had come back, minus his uniform and the war paint. Today, he looked heart-stoppingly handsome in jeans and a long-sleeved T-shirt that showed off his chest muscles.

"What's wrong? Did you leave something behind?"

He gave his head a little shake. "Yes—my sanity. I left it in Lympstone when I drove all the way over here, hoping a beautiful woman would agree to eat dinner with me even though she knows little more than my name."

"Sorry, what?"

He held up a bag. "I've brought takeout. Chinese and ice cream."

"Huh?" My words weren't working. "But why? I mean, why me?"

He closed the gap between us and rested his hands on my hips.

"Because you've got a good heart. That much is obvious from the way you look after Picky."

Picky had brought Matt back to me? I owed my pony a huge bag of carrots. "I want him to be happy."

"And I like a girl who takes chances then fights to win, the way you have with this house. It's a huge project, but you haven't given up, and the place has so much character."

He liked the house? Which parallel universe had I travelled to? I'd only taken a few leftover codeine tablets, for goodness' sake.

Matt tucked a lock of hair behind my ear, and I leaned into his touch without thinking about it. Wherever I'd ended up, I wanted to stay there when he leaned down and pressed his lips to my forehead.

"Sarah, will you have dinner with me?"

Even if I *was* dreaming, there was only one answer I could give.

"Yes, I'll have dinner with you."

"Thank goodness for that." His lips curved into a smile as he pulled back, eyes twinkling. "Sorry I scared you yesterday, but maybe fate had some crazy plan for us. Do you believe in fate?"

"I'm tempted."

"Glad to hear it." This time, his lips met mine. "Because I've never been so tempted by anyone in my life."

Houdini the Hamster

CHAPTER 1

AS THE LAST child left the classroom, I slumped down in my seat and surveyed the aftermath of the Loxton Academy's Christmas party—the kind of chaos that only twenty-three entitled eight-year-olds high on sugar and the promise of a fortnight off could create. Wrapping paper was strewn everywhere, some little brat had drawn a wonky reindeer on a table, and sticky orange soda dripped out of an overturned can.

I'd been well prepared for today by my colleagues. Horror stories of the traditional end-of-term party abounded in the staffroom—everything from a meltdown among five-year-olds over who got the last mince pie to a punch-up over which happy, jolly Christmas tunes to play in the background.

When I heard about the party, my first question had been, "Why? Why even hold a party if it's so awful?"

There had been six other teachers sipping tea around me at that moment, and every single one of them rolled their eyes.

"Tradition," Maria explained. "Mrs. Loxton hates change. That's also why she makes the kids wear those stupid straw hats in summer and the scratchy scarves in winter."

"And it's not like the kids'll do any work on the last

day, anyway," Tim added.

It was all right for him. He taught PE and therefore managed to escape the fun on the pretence of tidying the equipment cupboard.

And no, the children wouldn't do any work, but it was the twenty-second of December, and I still wanted to spend my evening watching the *Strictly Come Dancing* special and drinking wine rather than clearing up empty crisp packets and picking bits of pastry out of the ancient carpet.

When I first landed the job at the Loxton Academy, I'd been... No, thrilled was the wrong word for it. I'd been desperate. Desperate to get away from my old life. The school had a fantastic reputation and always topped the exam tables, but the harsh reality of dealing with spoilt rich kids every day had left me crying into my cocoa on more than one occasion.

"It's not all bad," Maria said. "Every year, the parents get more competitive over whose kid gives the best gifts. Last Christmas, I got three spa vouchers and a mountain bike."

"A bike?"

"Joey Thompson's father owns a nationwide chain of bicycle shops," Tim explained. "We all got bikes."

"I think I'd rather skip the party *and* the gifts."

I hadn't sat on a bike since I fell off and scraped my knees on my eighth birthday, and the idea of showing off my wobbly bits at a spa filled me with dread.

"Oh, Cara," Maria giggled. "Lighten up. It can't possibly be as bad as you think."

Yes. Yes, it could. And as I surveyed the aforementioned pile of gifts, which stretched from the edge of my desk all the way to the wall twenty feet away, I wondered how on earth I'd manage to fit everything into my Nissan Micra. I'd have to make at least four trips, and as for the surfboard...

"Miss Taylor?"

A quiet voice made me look up, and I saw Utah de Witt. Yes, his parents really named him that, and to make it worse, his middle name was Striker. Can you guess his daddy was a footballer? Utah himself was a sweet kid, though, a bookworm, and my favourite because he never caused trouble.

"Is something wrong?"

Mrs. de Witt flipped a curtain of blonde hair away from her face and teetered forwards on four-inch heels, carrying a box that looked to be two feet square. Oh dear. Tell me that wasn't another Christmas gift?

"Nothing's wrong, nothing at all. I just got delayed buying your Christmas present, so we've come to drop it off before we head to the airport."

"Are you going somewhere nice?"

"The Bahamas. I read an article last week that said tanning beds cause cancer, so we thought we'd go and lie in the sun instead."

Okaaaaay. "Well, have a lovely trip, and thanks so much for thinking of me."

"It was Utah's idea, wasn't it, sweetie?" She ruffled his hair, and he jerked his head away. "He overheard you telling one of the other teachers you'd be spending Christmas on your own, so we thought we'd get you a little friend."

Excuse me? "A...a friend?"

"Every girl needs one."

Her words washed over me as another wave of loneliness hit. Since my scummy ex-boyfriend moved in with my ex-best friend and I fled from my ex-home, I'd done my best to block out my past with boxes of chocolate and endless stacks of badly completed homework. I hadn't been looking forward to Christmas even in my brighter moments. Tears prickled behind my eyelids, but I blinked them away as Mrs. de Witt deposited the box on an empty desk and backed out of the door before I could ask any more questions. What on earth had she bought?

As I got nearer, a strange vibration came from the package, and it began to inch its way across the table. Surely not? She couldn't have meant a battery-operated boyfriend, could she? I mean, that box was massive.

The noise stopped, and I was tempted to walk right out of the door, away from the gifts and the mess and the piles of marking I was supposed to take home for the holidays. But then the package vibrated again, and curiosity got the better of me.

I tore open the paper to reveal a brown cardboard box, and when I flipped open the lid...

Freaking heck!

Pulse racing, I leapt back a foot and shrieked as two black eyes stared back at me. What was it?

Footsteps echoed down the corridor, and Maria skidded into the classroom.

"What's wrong? Are you okay? I heard a scream."

"It's...it's..." I pointed at the box.

She stepped forwards and peered into the top. "A hamster? Why have you got a hamster?"

"Uh, it's a Christmas gift?"

As well as the cage, Mrs. de Witt had included dried food, a bag of sawdust, and a packet of Royal Rodent Gourmet Apple Snax. How thoughtful. Meanwhile, the little ball of fluff kept running on his wheel, oblivious to the consternation he was causing.

"Good grief. Tristan Smythe gave me a ready-plucked pheasant from his father's estate, but I think this might actually be worse. What will you do with it?"

"I have no idea. At the moment, I'm just panicking."

"Haven't you had a pet before?"

"Except for a goldfish, no. My little brother was allergic to anything with fur."

The hamster climbed up the bars of the cage and poked his nose out, whiskers twitching as he took in the world beyond the box, and Maria and I both stepped back a pace.

"Now what?" I asked.

"Maybe you could take it back to the pet shop?"

"I don't even know where they bought it." I closed my eyes and sucked in a deep breath. "And I can't risk offending them, not when Utah's education costs five figures a term."

"Okay, okay. Google is your friend here." Maria tugged her phone out of her pocket. "Right, according to Wikipedia, hamsters can survive on a diet of commercial food." She peered into the box again. "Looks as if you've got that. And most hamsters like to live on their own. Poor little things. Do you reckon they get lonely?"

Probably, if my own experiences were anything to go by. I didn't know whether to be touched or insulted by Mrs. de Witt's efforts to set me up with a hamster instead of a boyfriend. A snort of laughter escaped, and Maria looked at me funny. Perhaps I could add my new-found interest in animals to my online dating profile? Let's face it, simply being a woman in her mid-twenties with a stable job and love of Netflix hadn't generated many clicks.

"I suppose I'll have to take it home."

"What are you gonna call it?"

"You really think that's the most important thing on my mind right now?"

"Hamlet? Ham Solo? Hambo?"

"What if it's a girl? How do you tell?"

"No idea." Maria leaned closer and squinted. "Is that a...? Never mind. I think it's a tail. How about Hamantha? Hamela Anderson?"

"Be serious," I said, but I was laughing.

"Do you need a hand out to your car with this lot?"

"I won't say no if you're offering. But honestly, what am I going to do with an electric guitar? I could barely play the recorder at school."

"Just sell anything you don't want on eBay. Last year, I made enough for a holiday to Lanzarote."

CHAPTER 2

THAT EVENING, I missed the finale of *Strictly Come Dancing* while I surfed the internet. Who knew you could buy so much cute stuff for hamsters? A sleeping pouch shaped like a giant strawberry, a tiny fort, even a little car for them to roll around in. Before I knew it, I'd ordered one of everything for Hammie, who peered down at me from the dining table in between stuffing her cheek pouches with food and running on her wheel. I'd started thinking of her as a girl, mainly because the way she twitched her nose reminded me of my Auntie Bernice, who suffered from chronic hay fever.

Although I had to admit, Hammie's little snuffles were a lot cuter.

"Maybe you're not so bad, little one," I told her that evening before I went to bed. After all, it wasn't her fault she'd been dumped on me. She just waggled her whiskers and stuffed another peanut into her cheeks.

That night, I found out one of the downsides of having a nocturnal pet. The noise. The flipping noise. I could cope with the rattling of the bars and Hammie scuffing through her food dish, but the vibrations from that bloody wheel went right through my core, and not in a good way.

I tried stuffing cotton wool in my ears and burying my head under the pillow, but it was no good. At five a.m., I stumbled out of the bedroom and removed the thing, much to Hammie's sadness.

"Oh, don't look at me like that."

Twitch. Twitch.

"It's just that I can't sleep."

Twitch. Twitch.

"You can have it back in the morning."

Except she'd be asleep then, wouldn't she? And what if she got fat through lack of exercise? Could hamsters suffer from obesity? A quick internet search suggested it was possible.

"I'll buy you a new wheel. A quieter one. How about that?"

Twitch. Twitch. Twitch.

CHAPTER 3

AT NINE A.M. on December twenty-third, I loaded myself up with caffeine and joined the Rodent World internet forum. And my first post?

Help! Do silent wheels exist?

I didn't expect to get many answers, but by the time I'd washed up my cereal bowl and stacked it back in the cupboard, the computer was pinging away as though it'd learned Morse code. Wow. Over twenty replies, and most of them recommended the "super-stealthy" wheel —a silver contraption that looked as if it came off a spaceship. The messages kept coming, welcoming me to the forum and asking about my pets.

I glanced over at Hammie's cage on the end of the dining table. She'd gone to sleep now, leaving a scattered trail of multicoloured hamster kibble in her wake.

Well, my parents brought me up to be polite, so I could hardly ignore these people, could I? I took a deep breath and tapped out my first message, a "thank you" for all the help so far.

By lunchtime, I'd got absolutely no preparation done for Christmas, but did have three recipes for home-made critter treats, detailed instructions on how to clean out Hammie's cage, and the address for my nearest stockist of stealthy wheels.

"Who knew a virtual community could be so helpful?" I muttered to myself as I opened a tin of soup for lunch.

Normally when I wasn't at school, the doldrums hit by noon, and I spent the afternoon curled up under a blanket, torturing myself by watching romcoms as I rued the sorry state of my love life. But this afternoon was different. Talking to new people, even via the computer, had pushed a little of the darkness away.

And I really, really needed to buy Hammie a new wheel in order to get some sleep tonight.

Penny's Pets was located in the next village, its bright front window filled with cat beds and dog treats and colourful hanging bird toys. The bell jangled as I pushed the door open, and when I got inside, animal chatter filled the air.

"Can I help?" the blonde lady behind the counter asked. Penny? Yes, according to her name badge.

She looked about my age, but her eyes still had that sparkle mine had lost when I walked in on the two most important people in my life doing the dirty with each other.

"I'm looking for a wheel."

"Hamster? Gerbil? Chinchilla? Sugar glider?"

"What's a sugar glider?"

She slipped out from behind the counter and led me over to a giant cage in the far corner. A fleecy pouch hung in one corner, and she reached inside and held it open so I could take a look. Aww! Two tiny creatures huddled inside, about the size of Hammie but with long tails and a black stripe down the middle of each of their backs.

"They're so cute! Are they similar to chipmunks?"

"Only in looks. They move more slowly, and they're actually marsupials rather than rodents. This pair are my personal pets. They come home with me each evening. What pets do you have?"

"Just one hamster." The whole story of Hammie and Utah de Witt came spilling out, and by the end of it, Penny was laughing like crazy. "So, you see, I need a new wheel so I don't lose my sanity."

"Well, you've certainly come to the right place. We've got wheels in all shapes and sizes. The super-stealthy wheel's pricey, but it's our best seller."

Pricey and big. "I'm not sure that'll even fit in the cage."

Penny sucked in a breath. "What are you keeping her in?"

"Uh, it's made from wire, about this big." I demonstrated with my hands.

"Hmm... You could do with something a bit larger for her to stay happy. What do you think of this one?"

So, it seemed that size mattered for rodent cages, just like certain other areas in life. And I did want Hammie to be happy.

"Okay, I'll take it. And perhaps a few extra toys?"

By the time Penny helped me to carry everything out to my car, I'd acquired the cage, the wheel, a blue plastic ball for Hammie to roll around in, and a thick book titled *The A-Z of Hamsters*. Between that lot and my eBay purchases, Hammie would need her own bedroom soon.

"Why don't you come to my next pet-lover's coffee morning?" Penny asked as I shut the lid of the boot. "I hold it on the first Saturday of the month in the café there." She pointed at Eats and Treats two doors up.

"I don't know..."

"If you're new to the area, it's a great way to meet people. And they're a nice bunch. When it first started, I thought ten people might show up, but at least forty come every month now."

Apart from school events, I hadn't done anything social since the *incident*, as I'd taken to calling it. And I knew my ex hadn't held back. In my blacker moments, I might have stalked him on Facebook, then cried a lot. Last week, he'd taken his nasty, back-stabbing new girlfriend on a minibreak to Paris. They'd climbed the Eiffel Tower, eaten dinner at a posh restaurant, and snapped selfies at Versailles while I spooned down Häagen-Dazs and wondered if I'd ever meet another man who wasn't A) eight years old, B) an irate father complaining that Tarquin had an ink stain on his trousers, or C) a colleague. I might have relaxed rule C if any of them had been vaguely attractive or even available, but Mrs. Loxton always hired men with rings on their fingers to stave off any rumours of impropriety.

Penny gave me a nudge. "Come on, you know you want to."

Maybe, just maybe, I'd meet some new friends. "Okay, I will."

Chapter 4

THAT EVENING, I gingerly lifted Hammie out of her inadequate cage and placed her in my lap. Penny had assured me that hamsters rarely bit hard, although she might have a little nibble just to see what I tasted like. I held out one of the Apple Snax.

"Hungry, little one?"

She took a bite, then grabbed the whole thing and stuffed it away in her cheeks. Cute. Once she'd run up and down my arm and, yes, taken a small chunk out of my thumb before turning her nose up in disgust, I loaded her into the ball to run around while I set up her shiny new home. For the moment, I'd moved it onto my coffee table. But I could buy Hammie her own table in the sales, and rearrange the furniture a bit, and... Okay, the idea of having a hamster was growing on me. I felt happier today than I had in months.

That good mood continued right the way through the next day while I chatted with my new online buddies and rounded up the ingredients for Christmas dinner. My parents were on a cruise, and my little brother was currently in the Antarctic doing research on sea ice, but I still wanted roast turkey.

And roast turkey I was going to get. Every day for the next month if Sainsbury's had anything to do with it. Special offers meant I ended up with a whole turkey, five kilos of potatoes, three jars of cranberry sauce, half a dozen melons, thirty-six mince pies, and a Christmas pudding the size of a football.

"Good thing I've got freezer space, isn't it?" I told Hammie as I stacked all the food away. My tiny semi-detached house only had two proper rooms downstairs, but I'd kept the family-sized fridge-freezer after my break-up and squeezed it in alongside the table and chairs I'd bought from IKEA.

Hammie didn't answer, of course, but when I went back into the living room, I found her running around in her new and thankfully silent wheel.

"Do you want to come out to play?" I asked, then rolled my eyes at myself because I was talking to a freaking hamster. Good grief.

I took her silence as a yes and laughed as she ran across my lap and up the arm of the sofa. So adorable. I set her down in my lap, only for her to repeat the manoeuvre, this time adding in a backflip at the top. Aw, she— Flipping heck! What was that? I stared in horror at the peanut-sized appendage protruding from her bottom as she struggled to right herself. Did Hammie have a tumour? Or some sort of prolapse? Quick—where was the nearest vet?

Fingers trembling, I consulted Google, then lifted Hammie back into her smaller cage and hurried out to the car. Sobs threatened to escape as I climbed in behind the wheel. I may have only had the little critter for a couple of days, but I'd grown quite attached.

The four-mile drive seemed to take forever, but we finally arrived at the Family Friends Veterinary Centre. A sign next to the doorbell said Press for Emergencies, and I held my finger down as my heart clawed its way up my throat.

Footsteps approached, and the door swung open.

"Can I help?"

I took in the man's white coat, his strong jaw, his tousled blond hair, his raised eyebrow. Holy hell, the vet was hot.

"I, uh, I've got a...a..."

"A hamster?" he prompted with a hint of a Scottish accent.

"Yes! A hamster."

"And...?"

"She's got a lump." A tear popped out unbidden. "Please, I don't want her to die."

"Okay, let's get her into the exam room. Do you want me to take the cage?"

I handed it over and stumbled inside behind the vet, and wow, he looked incredibly nice from the back too. Handsome in a preppy kind of way. An Abercrombie & Fitch model, maybe, or possibly Ralph —

"How long has she had the lump?"

"I'm not sure. I mean, I just noticed it this evening, but I've only had her for two days. She was a Christmas present."

The vet lifted poor Hammie out of her cage and flipped her over. "Show me where?"

I pointed, hardly able to look. Was I imagining it, or had it grown?

The vet's mouth quirked up at the corners, then his shoulders shook, and finally, he burst into laughter.

"What's so funny? My poor hamster's tumour is hardly a humorous matter."

"It's...it's not..." He couldn't even speak through the

guffaws. "It's not a tumour. Those are his...his genitals."

The surgery didn't have a mirror, but I imagine I must have turned the colour of Santa's outfit.

"She's a he?"

"Definitely."

"No. No way. They're enormous."

"Yup."

"But if he was a human, they'd...they'd..." I trailed off. Yes, I'd embarrassed myself quite enough already, thank you very much.

"Be down to his knees?"

Please, floor, open up and swallow me.

"Could we pretend we never had this conversation?"

The vet put Hammie back in her—his—cage and gripped the sides of the table as he laughed harder.

"No way. This is the best emergency visit I've ever had."

That was entirely a matter of opinion. And what made it worse, he looked even sexier when he grinned. Little dimples popped out, and I almost said something else stupid just to keep him smiling.

"Uh, maybe I should go now."

"While you're here, I might as well give the little chap a check over. You know, to set your mind at ease."

I stared at the floor while the vet retrieved Hammie again. Dammit—the first desirable man I'd spoken to in months, and I'd ballsed things up totally. Calamity Cara, that was what my little brother used to call me, and I'd certainly lived up to my billing.

"Everything looks good," the vet said.

"Thank you so much. How much do I owe you?"

"I should be paying *you* for the entertainment."

"I'm sorry I wasted your time, and so close to Christmas as well."

"Better to bring a pet in unnecessarily than ignore a potential problem. If anything else worries you, just give me a call." He fished a business card out of his pocket and flashed a smile. "Anytime."

The way he said that, it was almost as if he was... flirting?

No way. Not with such a monumental idiot.

"Well, I really should be going. Presents to wrap, wine to drink, that sort of thing."

Great, now I'd made myself sound like an alcoholic.

"I'll get the door for you." He held it while I tried to walk out with a few shreds of dignity intact. "See you around."

CHAPTER 5

ONCE I'D REPLACED Hammie in his cage on the coffee table, I stayed true to my word. After three large glasses of red, I passed out on the sofa, dead to the world. In my dreams, I peeled the sexy vet out of his lab coat while he gave me a lecture on hamster behaviour in that delightful accent of his. So *Scottish*. I nodded, barely taking in a word as he bent me over the examination table and...and...then I woke up.

Boo.

The first thing I did was glance out the window to check for snow, but of course, there wasn't any. A sprinkling of rain pitter-pattered against the window while grey clouds hovered overhead. Good thing I didn't have to go out today, wasn't it? No, I had the whole day to prepare an extra Christmas dinner because, let's face it, I'd be eating turkey well into January otherwise. And in the afternoon, I could watch *The Sound of Music* and stuff myself silly on chocolate and mince pies. But first, I needed paracetamol to get rid of my headache. Had the dull throb been caused by last night's embarrassment or the alcohol?

"Happy Christmas Eve, Hammie," I muttered, rolling off the sofa and heading for the kitchen.

I should bring him something tasty for breakfast. Were hamsters allowed to eat cranberries? Or mince pies? In the end, I opted for one more Apple Snax. The last thing I needed was another trip to the vet, although my libido disagreed with me there.

"Here you go, little dude." I opened the cage and poked the treat through the window of his tiny house. "Hungry?"

Nope, it appeared not.

No rustle of bedding. No twitching nose.

Was Hammie okay? I lifted the roof and found... nothing. No Hammie. My stomach lurched into my mouth. Where on earth had he gone?

I poked around in the cage, even checking under his food bowl just in case he'd shrunk. But he'd disappeared, and worse, I realised the side door half-hidden behind the stealthy wheel was hanging open. I flopped onto the sofa and groaned. He'd escaped, hadn't he? The little git had made a break for it.

Now, when the estate agent showed me around the house, he'd been almost apologetic about the size, and certainly it had never seemed spacious. But trust me, when you're hunting for a creature the size of your fist, even a shoebox seems enormous. I spent Christmas Eve tearing the place apart from the front door to the back door and rummaging through the bedroom and bathroom upstairs.

Nothing.

Hammie had vanished. I glanced through the window and into the garden, where the rain had turned to sleet. He couldn't have got outside, could he? A draught seeped in under the front door, reminding me how chilly it was. Please, say he'd just curled up somewhere warm and gone to sleep.

As darkness fell, I laid out little dishes of food in

case they tempted him from his hiding place, then set up camp on the sofa with a torch. Hammie was nocturnal, right? So it stood to reason he'd make an appearance.

"Come on, little buddy. Your wheel's waiting."

But silence reigned all around, at least until four a.m. when a quiet scratching woke me up. Hammie? Where was it coming from? I traipsed around the house, pausing to listen every few seconds to see if I was any closer. By five a.m., I let out a low groan. The noise was coming from the living room floor. *The freaking floor.*

I knelt and pressed an ear to the carpet. Yes, something was definitely under there, and unless a mouse had taken up residence, it had to be Hammie. I rocked back on my heels and tore at my hair. How had he even got down there?

And, more importantly, how was I going to get him out?

At nine a.m., I was wondering whether I could pry up floorboards with a nail file when my phone trilled on the coffee table. Mum and Dad? My brother? No, Maria.

"I just thought I'd call and wish you a happy Christmas," she said.

A sweet thought, but her voice held a hint of pity. After all, it was Maria who Utah de Witt had overheard me telling that I'd be spending Christmas alone.

"Oh, er, thanks. Happy Christmas to you too."

"How's the hamster? Did you give her a name yet?"

"Him. I know that much now. And he's escaped."

"What? How?"

"Partly wine, partly incompetence." The whole story

came spilling out, from Rodent World to Penny's Pets to the disaster at the vet's. "Without a doubt, this is the most embarrassing week of my life. And how am I supposed to get a hamster out from under the floor? I don't even own a screwdriver."

"Can't help with tools, I'm afraid, and my Derek doesn't know a hammer from a chisel." She snapped her fingers. "Got it! Why don't you call the fire brigade?"

"Why? I haven't started cooking anything yet."

"They rescue cats in trees, don't they? Surely they'll help out with a hamster."

"I can't call 999 because my hamster's gone missing."

"The fire station's only two streets away from your house. Just nip around there and borrow a pry bar or something."

"Are you crazy? I can't just walk into a building full of men and admit to yet another moment of utter idiocy. I'm going to throttle Mrs. de Witt in January."

"Why? She wanted to get you a friend. Now you've got your new online buddies, a coffee morning with that Penny girl to look forward to, and a hot vet who may be interested. I'd say she's done pretty well."

"When you put it like that..."

"Happy Christmas, and good luck with the firemen."

CHAPTER 6

BY LUNCHTIME, I'D tried and failed to lift a floorboard using the socket set from the boot of my car, and embarked on a fruitless search to find a DIY store open on Christmas Day. I may have also shed a few tears and finished off the bottle of wine.

And now, I admitted defeat.

If I wanted Hammie back, I'd have to go with Maria's ridiculous plan. I checked my hair in the mirror, put on a touch of lipstick, stuck my feet into my trainers, and set off along the road to the fire station, feeling sicker with every step. Why me? Was it bad karma? Payback for making Phillip Woodside play the back end of a donkey in the nativity play because he'd been annoying me all term?

My finger shook as I pressed the bell outside the fire station's reception, and I almost turned around and ran home. I'd taken two steps back when the door swung open.

"Can I help?"

I looked up. And up. Wow. The guy was a foot taller than me and made the vet look kind of ugly. Dark hair, a chiselled jaw with a smattering of stubble, and judging by the way his maroon T-shirt stretched across his chest, he spent all his spare time in the gym.

"I...uh..."

"Look, if Andy sent you, the boss got really pissed last time, so you'll have to leave."

"Andy? Who's Andy?"

"My brother. He sent us a stripper last Christmas. His idea of a joke."

I gasped. "I am *not* a stripper!"

His gaze travelled lazily up and down my body. "Well, not in that outfit."

Ouch. Okay, so I'd dressed for comfort rather than style, but his words still hurt. "I think I'll just leave."

I turned, but he stopped me with a hand on my shoulder. "Sorry. I didn't mean that the way it sounded. I just meant, well, you've got a nice figure."

Butterflies fluttered in my stomach. No, not butterflies. Peacocks. "I don't quite know what to say to that."

Thankfully, the arrival of a second fireman broke the awkward silence. He wasn't quite as sexy as the first, but his eyes twinkled.

"What's the problem?"

Deep breath. "My hamster escaped. And he's under the floor, and I don't have any tools, and I was wondering if you might have one of those claw hammers I could borrow?"

Once they'd finished laughing, the sexy guy grinned. "How about I go one better and prove I'm not the arsehole you think I am? It's shift change in ten minutes. I'll come around and help you."

"What about your family? It's Christmas."

A black look flickered across his face, but only for a second before his smile ratcheted up again. The sight of those pearly white teeth made me go quite dizzy.

"I don't have anywhere else to be, and it won't take

long. I'm Chris, by the way."

"Cara."

He held out his hand, and when mine touched it, a spark buzzed along my arm as my stomach did a backflip. Vet? What vet?

"We'll all help," Chris's friend said. "I had a hamster when I was a kid. Slippery little bugger—he was always escaping. We found him in the chimney one time."

"At least I don't have a chimney."

And that was how, an hour later, my living room was filled with six hot and slightly sweaty firemen, one of them minus a T-shirt, and half of my floor was missing. The musky smell of man permeated through the house, and I concentrated on my breathing so I didn't start panting. Hot damn. *Happy Christmas, Cara.*

Chris leaned forwards on his knees, shining a torch into the darkness. I took a moment to admire the way his trousers clung to his well-muscled backside and tried not to smile too widely. *Thanks, Hammie.* This was the best Christmas gift ever.

"There he is," Chris said. "Come here, little fella."

He reached down and scooped up a sleepy Hammie, who at that moment I decided to rename Houdini. It seemed appropriate. Chris's hand touched mine again as he passed the hamster over, and that spark crackled once more, stronger this time. Did Chris feel it too?

"Don't suppose you've got a coffee?" one of his friends asked, breaking the moment. "I'm parched."

"Sure. Right away."

And thank goodness for special offers, because I had enough deluxe deep-filled mince pies for five each.

Houdini barely stirred as the firemen began to hammer my floor back together, while I focused on bulging biceps and flexing abs. If only I could have taken photos, because this was a moment to treasure. I almost wished I'd bought myself a gerbil too.

But twenty minutes later, the carpet was back in place, and the men trooped out. All except Chris, anyway.

"You need a few more nails in those floorboards. I could come over next week and fix it if you like?"

His initial cockiness had subsided, and as he looked down at me, his flickering smile made him look a little...nervous?

"Are you sure?"

"Wouldn't have offered otherwise."

"In that case, I'd really appreciate it."

"After my shift on Tuesday? About three o'clock?"

"Perfect. I'm off work all next week."

He drained the last of his coffee, but the selfish part of me didn't want him to leave.

"Can I get you another cup? Or a mince pie?" A nervous giggle popped out. "Christmas dinner?"

"You're not spending the rest of today with anyone? Family? A boyfriend?"

I shook my head, perhaps a bit harder than necessary, then sank onto the sofa. "I don't have a boyfriend."

"Really?"

Chris sounded surprised, and that made me smile despite thoughts of my ex.

"We split up, and I moved here to get away from the memories. I don't know many people in the area yet."

Chris sat down beside me, elbows on his knees.

"Same. Except it was a girlfriend, and she's now living with my ex-best mate." He turned his head and gave me a sheepish smile. "I've got a pizza for Christmas dinner."

How could anyone have ditched this man? Okay, so he'd been slightly rude at first, but underneath he had a heart of gold. Plus the added bonus of looks that could stop traffic. And right now, he was in my house, and I kind of wanted him to stay there.

"I accidentally bought enough turkey and veg to feed ten people, so how about I cook?" I suggested, hardly daring to hope. "At least if I burn anything, you're in the right profession."

Chris smiled again, and this time it reached his eyes. "I'd like that, Cara." My skin tingled as he took my hand and gave it a gentle squeeze. "I'd like that a lot."

Freaking heck! The man was way out of my league, but he said *yes*!

I began fanning myself, realised what I was doing, and hastily used my fingers to tuck a stray lock of hair behind my ear instead.

"I'd better get cracking. Melon to start with?"

"I'll give you a hand."

And as we rose to our feet, that hand rested on the small of my back. A delicious shiver ran through me as I headed to the kitchen, muttering thanks to Houdini, Utah de Witt, and Maria as Chris followed close behind.

Perhaps this Christmas hadn't turned out so bad after all.

Wʜᴀᴛ's ɴᴇxᴛ?

If you want to see more of Nate and Carmen, they also appear in my Blackwood Security series, starting with *Pitch Black*.

Even a Diamond can be shattered...

After the owner of a security company is murdered, his sharp-edged wife goes on the run. Forced to abandon everything she holds dear - her home, her friends, her job in special ops - she builds a new life for herself in England. As Ashlyn Hale, she meets Luke, a handsome local who makes her realise just how lonely she is.

Yet, even in the sleepy village of Lower Foxford, the dark side of life dogs Diamond's trail when the unthinkable strikes. Forced out of hiding, she races against time to save those she cares about. But is it too little, too late?

Find out more and pick up your FREE copy here:
www.elise-noble.com/pitch-black

The next Blackwood book will be *Shallow Graves*, in the Blackwood UK series.

To plant a garden is to believe in the future, that's what Dove Hallam's grandmother always told her. But at twenty-two, Dove has neither. Stuck in a dead-end relationship and a job she hates, her life is going nowhere until she meets Marlene Grande.

Although Marlene is in her seventies, her appetite for hot men and spending money knows no bounds, even if her matchmaking skills leave a bit to be desired. But as Dove embraces her new life, someone isn't so keen on her having fun.

Marlene's solution? Hire a private investigator with a nice ass. Now Dove has two problems to deal with—the monster wreaking havoc on the Arndale estate and Zander Graves, a smart-mouthed womaniser she really doesn't want to like.

Will there be anything left of her heart by the time they've finished with it?

Find out more here: www.elise-noble.com/graves

If you enjoyed For the Love of Animals, please consider leaving a review.

For an author, every review is incredibly important. Not only do they make us feel warm and fuzzy inside, readers consider them when making their decision whether or not to buy a book. Even a line saying you enjoyed the book or what your favourite part was helps a lot.

Want to stalk me?

For updates on my new releases, giveaways, and other random stuff, you can sign up for my newsletter on my website:
www.elise-noble.com

Facebook:
www.facebook.com/EliseNobleAuthor

Twitter: @EliseANoble

Instagram: @elise_noble

I also have a group on Facebook for my fans to hang out. They love the characters from my Blackwood and Trouble books almost as much as I do, and they're the first to find out about my new stories as well as throwing in their own ideas that sometimes make it into print!

And if you'd like to read my books for FREE, you can also find details of how to join my review team.

Would you like to join Team Blackwood?

www.elise-noble.com/team-blackwood

END OF BOOK STUFF

Last November, I visited Dahab, Egypt in what's become something of an annual pilgrimage for me. I go for the scuba diving, which is some of the best in the world, but also for the amazing weather and the super friendly people who live there. That part of the world's had a bad time in the media lately, but I consider myself lucky to be able to go there and see what it's really like. Sure, there are a few assholes just like everywhere else, but on the whole, I feel safer walking down the street in Dahab than in London or Paris or any other western city, and Dahabians go above and beyond to make visitors feel welcome. They have a saying—come as a guest, leave as a friend—and it's so true.

You want an example? A couple of years ago, my other half dropped his wallet there. He realised an hour or so later when he went to pay for dinner, and when we backtracked our steps, nobody had seen it, but one of the shops we'd been into was closed. Panic set in. Then people started pointing at me. It turned out the owner of the closed shop had found the wallet, and it had a picture of me in it, so he set out searching.

A taxi driver recalled picking me up from the Hilton, so they went there, and when I hadn't arrived back yet, the receptionist photocopied my picture and they started distributing it all through town. Soon everyone was helping to hook me up with shop dude and taxi dude, who were still riding around looking for me. They all celebrated the reunion, and days later, people were still asking about the wallet.

Anyhow, I digress—if you want to read more tales of Egyptian craziness, you can find those in *Trouble in Paradise*, but I should be talking about animals here.

I'd seen stories on Facebook about Janet's Wadi, an animal sanctuary based in a wadi (a dried up riverbed) in Dahab. The town's full of animals—camels, horses, goats, dogs, and cats—but many of the dogs are stray and every so often, the government likes to have a purge. For the dogs, that involves poison (see the aforementioned assholes).

So a few years ago, an English lady called Janet decided to set up a safe haven where they could live in peace, and along the way, she ended up with a few cats and horses too. And a donkey called Bimbo.

I wanted to make a donation, so I met up with Janet and she took me to see the animals. First, we visited the stables, where I was impressed by the condition of the horses. Often they look a bit thin out there because food is expensive and has to be trucked in, and thanks to the scare stories all over the internet, tourism has declined hugely in recent years so money's tight. But Janet's horses were the healthiest I'd seen. And curled up in a pile of berseem, the clover they feed the animals in Egypt, was Gigi, a dainty black and white dog who was staying there because she had a penchant for escaping from everywhere else.

And when we left to visit the wadi, she—you've guessed it—escaped and came with us, riding in the jeep as we drove up the coast. Night had fallen by the time we arrived, and I've never seen such a beautiful sky. With no light pollution or clouds, all the stars were visible, and I could have looked at it for hours.

But then we turned our torches on, and about two-hundred eyes gleamed back at us like something out of a horror movie. I've never seen so many dogs in one place, and soon they were leaping all around Janet, tails wagging. It was clear how much they all loved her, and also surprising how they all lived in harmony in their desert home.

The wadi is truly a special place.

A special place that's run on a shoestring by Janet and a team of volunteers, who have to raise enough money to provide food and water each month (water has to be brought in by a tanker), as well as rehoming animals whenever they can—a thankless task made all the more difficult by the Egyptian economy.

That night, I wanted to buy Janet dinner as a small token of *my* appreciation for all she did for the animals, and of course, Gigi invited herself along too. Dogs are welcome in most of the restaurants, and she curled up on a spare seat and went to sleep, happy to be around people.

I didn't think I'd ever see her again, but fast forward to the beginning of this year and Janet messaged me to say she really wanted Gigi to have a home in the UK. She kept escaping, and it was only a matter of time before she came across poison. Her partner in crime, Skinny, had already died on one of his excursions, and nobody wanted the same to happen to Gigi.

So I said I'd take her.

Talk about a logistical challenge—first a taxi ride from Dahab to Sharm el Sheikh, then a flight to Cairo with Janet, a night in the airport's cargo village, and finally a trip to Heathrow Airport with only a spaniel for company. Two days of travelling, and now Gigi's in her new home, but there are still many animals who need help.

And that's where this book comes in.

I wrote Nate and Carmen's story during the same trip I met Gigi on, so it seemed only fitting to donate the proceeds from all the sales to Janet's Wadi to help other dogs, including three of Gigi's puppies, who still live there. By buying this book, you've contributed towards helping them, so thank you.

Thank you also to Abigail Sins for contributing her time to design the cover, and to Nikki for bumping me up the editing queue to get the book out quickly. And thanks as always to my awesome beta readers—Cecilia, Quenby, Nikita, Jessica, Stacia, David, Musi, Lina, Terri, Renata, and Jeff, especially Musi for checking my Spanish! And thank you to my proof readers, Lizbeth and John.

My next release will be Shallow Graves, the third full-length novel in the Blackwood UK series, starring Zander and Dove—hope to chat with you again soon!

Elise

Roses are Dead
Shallow Graves (2018)
Indigo Rain (TBA)

The Electi Series
Cursed (2018)
Spooked (2018)
Possessed (TBA)

The Trouble Series
Trouble in Paradise
Nothing but Trouble
24 Hours of Trouble

Standalone
Life
For the Love of Animals (Blackwood prequel)
A Very Happy Christmas (novella)
Twisted

Printed in Great Britain
by Amazon